THE BIG SCORE

Karen & Isabella Tucci

True Heart Romance

Contents

Free Book   V

Karen's Other Books: VI

Authors' Note   VIII

1   1

2   6

3   16

4   22

5   31

6   43

7   52

8   61

9   68

10   72

11   80

12   84

13   91

14   97

15   104

16	110
17	116
18	123
19	131
20	137
21	144
22	147
23	151
24	161
25	167
26	172
27	179
28	185
29	193
30	199
31	205
32	207
33	210
34	214
How About a Review?	221
About the Author	222

Free Book

Karen's Other Books:

Stand Alone Books:

<u>When the Dust Settles: A Sweet Romance with a Navy SEAL</u>

G & G Security Series (Coming 2025)

(The characters from When the Dust Settles cross-over in this series)

Operation: Heal my SEAL Book 1

Operation: Find my SEAL Book 2

Operation: Keep my SEAL Book 3

Operation: Train my SEAL Book 4

Second Chance Series:

<u>Starting Over</u>

<u>Moving On</u>

<u>Together Again</u> Free with NL sign up

Big L' Ranch Series

The Perfect Kiss: Book 1

The Perfect: Cowboy Book 2

The Perfect Match Book 3

The Perfect Christmas (Holiday Novella)

The Perfect Sheriff Book 5

Best Friends Series

Let Me Carry YouFree with NL sign up

Let Me Marry You

YA Cumberland Christian Prep School Series

The Big Score

Authors' Note

HIGH SCHOOL IS HARD. Most people, when asked, have said they'd never return to that time of their life. As you read about the teens from Cumberland Christian Academy, the Saints' soccer team's home, you'll see that they endure the same drama as teens and adults IRL (In Real Life). They have strained relationships, potential danger lurking over them, and they let romantic feelings, and anxiety impact their decisions.

They say that the best books are 98% truth and 2% fiction. Many people read to escape the complexity of life and we believe it's possible to do that with this story, but reality has a way of creeping in and the writing becomes a mechanism for healing. As a teenager, Isabella has weathered many of the situations you're about to read. Obviously, we've changed names and altered scenes to make them fit the story line. That said, it's our hope that we captured each situation in the least severe way possible, allowing all readers to tolerate every scene. In our opinion, chapter 14 may be the hardest chapter to read if you are triggered by out-of-control teenagers at a party. It brings us peace, knowing there is a HEA in this book and real life. With God, forgiveness and love are possible in spite of the darkness of the world. We hope you enjoy this non-spicy YA soccer romance and fall in love with Nik and Keeley.

ANOTHER ITEM TO ADDRESS: Teenage lingo. This changes with the generations, so while most of it's easy to figure out in context, we've included a glossary of sorts for your convenience.

Bussin' - something cool, great, awesome

Flex - to show off, boast about something

FR - for real

G.O.A.T – Greatest of all time

Lit - exciting, excellent

No cap - no lie

Smack - criticizing a person behind their back

Sus - suspicious

Simp - someone who shows excessive attention toward another person

Finally, when you see their texts, the punctuation is sporadic or completely missing to replicate true teen's texts. It pained me (Karen) not to use punctuation, so I left the texting parts to Isabella. Happy Reading!

Blessings,

Karen and Isabella Tucci

1

Sicily, Italy

"Hurry up, Keeley." I checked my watch for the fifth time in the last two minutes. I never thought she'd abandon me... yet here I am standing by our tree waiting for her to show. It's not the prettiest tree, but two years ago, just one week after we met, Keeley selected this one to write our initials on. She said, "When you look at it, Mount. Etna lays in the backdrop, smoking and grumbling as it watches over the city just like you've watched over me."

She has a way with words. Like the time she told me I was her hero and protector. I know those words aren't like Shakespeare's, but my heart still swells whenever I relive that moment. So, like the fool I am, I keep extending how long I'll wait in the humid weather. My skin is crying, making my shirt cling to the damp spots. It's rather unusual for the sky to appear murky during July. People come to Sicily this time of year for the warm, sunny weather. But today, the gray clouds hang heavy and low as if they are pregnant with foreseeable rain. (If it does rain, it will be a wet ride back to town on my Vespa, but Keeley is worth every potential raindrop in the sky).

It won't rain though. I can't remember the last time it rained here in July. My eyes searched the roadway for as far as they could see. Squinting in both directions, trying to see even just one more kilometer if possible, but I came up empty. The road void of the cutest brunette on a white and black Vespa. I do, however, smile at just the thought of her and the rides we've taken together.

Why didn't her dad retire like he could have? Then Keeley could have stayed here. Who am I kidding? Even if the commander did retire, he had forbidden Keeley to see me. That's why we need to meet so far from town.

The incessant ticking of my watch vibrates in my chest and thumps in my ears. My feet have a mind of their own, pacing back and forth, avoiding the exposed tree roots. The wind sings, tricking me into thinking Keeley has arrived. With the excitement of a kid on Christmas, I rush to the clearing, only to have disappointment drown me in a sea of sorrow. Why hasn't she come?

Another glance at my watch fills me with angst. If I don't deliver this package for my dad before five o' clock... let's just say I better, shuddering to think about the consequences if I don't. I only have five more minutes, then I have to go. *Please God, bring Keeley to me!* Dad's been in a foul mood lately and the last thing I want to do is upset him.

I rub the necklace between my forefinger and thumb, the rivets on the outside contrast with the smooth golden heart in the middle. It's possible she can't get away. See, my dad forbade me to see her, too. Why? We still don't know.

For Keeley and I everything is straightforward. We like spending time with each other. I think she likes me just as much as I like her.

She lays her head on my shoulder often. Other times, she's touching my arms, while telling me that soccer players don't have this much muscle. A real ego booster for sure.

Back at our tree, I run my fingers over our initials. If she only knew how many times I thought of kissing her... Not only here, but everywhere. For the past two years, we have seen each other every day at school. Outside of our academics we've had a blast swimming in the Mediterranean Sea, hiking Mount Etna, snorkeling, and scuba diving. We also got our AM driver's license when we turned fourteen, allowing us to drive our 45 km/h Vespas.

For the past year we've had the freedom to drive anywhere our Vespa's would take us, but with the lingering fear in me, I still hadn't told her how I felt about her. In fact, I promised myself that I'd tell her today. Why did everything have to be so complicated?

My heart races when my phone pings with a text message. *Thank you, God, Keeley is on her way.*

That thought is short-lived. When I see my dad's name at the bottom of my screen, my first reaction is to throw it against a tree. Instead, like the dutiful son I am, I swipe my finger across the screen, pulling up his message.

Dad: Remember to get my package to the address I gave you before five. No excuses!

"Yes, Sir," I mock as I give him a thumbs up reaction. He hates that, which makes me smile. I'm not normally a rebellious kid, but I don't understand why he wants to keep Keeley away from me.

For weeks he's said I couldn't see her anymore because she is too good and will keep me from taking my place in the family business one day. What does that even mean? She's sweet; even when her dad is mean to her. Keeley is the first to help others out. To me, she sounds like the girl I want as my future wife.

I can take over the family business and have a wife. What's the family business? I'm not exactly sure. My dad tells me he's a boss and gets to order others around all day. That might sound like fun, but I'm not sure that's for me. I think I might want to play soccer.

Her dad said I was a bad influence; that he'd heard things about my dad. I still don't know what those things are and Keeley hasn't told me. I wonder if he's being honest. I didn't tell Keeley, but her dad controls her and she doesn't even know it. Did Keeley believe the bad things her dad said about his? *No, she couldn't.* My dad may be a lot of things, but he works hard to support his family, so the thought of someone speaking poorly of him doesn't sit well with me.

Apparently God is angry, too. At that moment of thought the sky opens up and a curtain of rain unleashes on me. Moments later the wind smacks me in the face... That was the exact wake up call I needed—she isn't coming, but do I listen? Of course not. A nervous drumbeat of hope hammers against my ribs, anchoring me to this spot.

"She'll show," I say out loud, hoping to change the mysterious weather and the probable ending I'd like to avoid.

I fall into the memory of my last conversation with my dad; it hadn't gone well. The recollection pounds at my brain just as hard as the rain pounds down on me now.

"But I love her, Dad. You can't keep us apart."

His sinister laugh waves through my mind, stirring up the anger all over again. "You're too young to know what love is."

Wrong. I love Keeley's butterscotch hair. When she braids it, I know she means business—always challenging me to one on one soccer battles. I love her green eyes that remind me of the Mediterranean Sea. When I gaze into them, I feel like I'm home. I have a strong urge to protect her from the world, but mostly her dad and the losers we go to school with. They're always flirting with her. I don't blame them, but they aren't right for her—I am.

A cracking tree branch behind me whips me back to the present as a red squirrel, probably looking for dry shelter, scurries through the forest, alerting me of the time. Six minutes have passed. *Already?* Time never slows down when you need it to.

Unable to wait any longer, I sigh and hang her locket around our branch, hoping she'll come get it later. I grip the heart with my hand and squeeze my eyes shut. Not only do I know what love is, but thanks to today, I know what a broken heart feels like. A sharp, burning sensation sears my chest and waves of nausea roll through my stomach. I refrain from puking in our spot.

"Goodbye, Keeley." I kiss the locket and say a quick prayer about seeing her again one day... God willing, when we are older and can make decisions for ourselves. I will come find you. You are my forever and always, my best friend and one day I'll make you my wife.

Thank you God for the rain. Only you and I will know how much water is from the clouds and how much is from my tears.

2

KEELEY JAMES—PRESENT DAY

EASTLAND, MAINE, AMERICA

I wish to formally voice my complaint—being the new kid sucks!

I am a pro; however, since I'm about to start my Junior year at another new school. How many schools have I attended? Seventeen! Thinking about my dad's comment this morning when he peeked into my room, makes me grip the steering wheel a little tighter as I turn into the school parking lot.

"Don't act all weird here so the kids don't like you."

Right. Like it's my fault people my age do whatever it takes to fit in, and instead of going along with them, I choose to walk away to stay in the good graces of my Savior. Then he criticizes and yells at me, telling me I can't turn my back on "my friends" and need to give them grace. Yet, he never has grace for me. In fact, when my doctor diagnosed me with anxiety, he had a few choice words for the doctor and said it was all in my head and I needed to get over it. I probably wouldn't have developed anxiety if I wasn't always trying to please him. Fortunately, I realized there is no pleasing him and I stopped trying, but that's only made him worse. I miss the days I was a fun bubbly person, like when I was around Nik.

"At least the sign is welcoming and their soccer field is bussin'," my brother EJ, short for Ethan Joseph, says from the passenger seat.

He isn't wrong. The Saint mascot above the fancy lettering of Cumberland Christian Prep School did *appear* neighborly. I shove my memory about my dad away and roll into the next one. This sign is much better than the roaring tiger that greeted us at our last school, mirroring almost every girl in that building. Cross them and their claws will extend, leaving your face scarred and your self-esteem shattered. Don't ask me how I know.

"Yeah, I guess."

"Come on Kee, don't get into a funk again. You did this the last time we moved."

I side-eyed him. He knew very well this wasn't like the last time. Leaving the land-locked midwest was nothing compared to leaving the Mediterranean and Nikolaus.

"It's not my fault he didn't write." My brother's tone held compassion we siblings reserve for the most important situations. I'm grateful.

"No, but it is your fault I didn't get to see him before we left Italy."

"Are we back at that again? I didn't tell dad to take your Vespa that day."

My little brother is right again, and the smug look on his face says it all. Talk about a bitter pill to swallow.

I'm convinced that Dad left me stranded that day on purpose, so I couldn't see Nik one more time. I wanted to tell him that he was very special to me. Two years later, even though we haven't had any contact, my heart still calls for him.

I still don't know why my dad disapproved of me hanging out with Nik. He only made a big deal about it the last two weeks of our time in Sicily. That was the same time he started discouraging me about my choice in music and clothing. Even my mom couldn't figure out what his deal was since it was clean music and modest shorts and shirts.

Pulling into a parking spot, I cut the engine with a push of the button, the silence broken only by the wild thumping of my heart against my ribs. I reach for the pendant hanging around my neck. It brings me back to a more pleasant time—one I remember fondly and my heart slowly returns to a normal rhythmic beating. My dad eventually returned my Vespa and yes, it was mine. I paid for it with money I'd saved. I paid for the gas and insurance... but I digress because it was years ago. It took me an hour to get to our spot, longer than it normally would have taken me. People must have been driving with caution due to the odd weather that day.

When I reached our special tree, I traced our initials, knowing I'd missed him. The sun shone after an unusual rain storm in the exact direction for the gold chain to reflect off its rays. Nik had left me a locket. Inside, he added a picture of us standing in front of the elephant fountain.

"Come on, Keeley, I don't want to be late." EJ throws my door open. *When did he get out?*

"Sorry, I was..."

"I know, thinking about Nikolaus."

I couldn't see, but I knew my cheeks were pink. The heat radiating from them kept me warm on this chilly September morning.

EJ is Mr. Popularity wherever we land, so starting a new school is nothing to him. Me, not so much. Since my fateful last day in Italy, I'm all about speaking my mind now, and if you don't like it, tough. I don't go looking for trouble, but somehow it always seems to find me, like I'm the North Star or something.

I also developed other nuisances. My chest burns the closer I get to the school's double doors. They're calling my name like Ursula beckons Ariel. Yes, I'm a Disney fan, but mainly the classics.

"Do you think we'll be here the rest of our high school careers, or at least mine?" I ask my brother, wishing he'd slow down. We both had the easy gait of an athlete, but one of his strides is two of mine. I'm not short; he's a full-grown man as a sophomore.

He lifts his hand to his forehead to shade his eyes from the blinding sun. It doesn't take long to see what's captured his attention. A group of girls approach from the side. "I sure hope so."

I backhand his arm and he puts on a show pretending it hurts. "You're such a boy."

"Hey! There's nothing boy about me," EJ feigns being upset with my choice of words and bumps my shoulder, knocking my bag to my elbow.

"Whatever," I say, rolling my eyes and hiking my backpack strap higher on my shoulder.

The girls sidled up to EJ. Of course, now he stops. The blonde with wavy blonde hair and more makeup than she needs loops her arm through my brothers, bats her eyelashes, and giggles at everything he says. He's eating this up. What's the issue with the male population? The girls' phoniness is obvious. Keeley's seen girls all around the world act like this. Her heart goes out to these girls, who undoubtedly lack self-confidence.

I guess that's another good thing about not getting sucked into groups or cliques, I can sit back and watch everything unfold, while saying a prayer of gratitude that it doesn't involve me. Except, at some point, I will probably feel the impact like I have in the past. Girls, similar to the ones swarming EJ, ridiculed me for having muscular legs and shoulders. I know I'm not paper thin, I can stand on my own without falling all over the nearest boy; not that a boy has ever offered.

I shake my head, not wanting to relive my painful past. "EJ, we have to get going," I huff, hoping these Barbie wannabes leave my brother alone.

"Who's she?" The girl's sticky sweet voice is off putting. When EJ faces me, she wrinkles her nose like I am yesterday's garbage, making my chest burn. I can't stand mean girls. Blood races through my veins.

I inhale, looping my arm through EJ's. As I exhale, I smile and say, "I'm his sister, so I'll be around a lot longer than you."

My brother lets me pull him away. "Come on EJ, you have better taste than that."

He ignores everything I say about girls. "It wouldn't hurt you to be a little more friendly, Keeley. You've got to start trusting people again."

If it were only that easy. I'm sorry, Lord, for my judgy thoughts. "Yeah, maybe." In my experience the people who put on a show in front of others are the ones to trust the least. EJ doesn't see it with Dad and he didn't see it with the beautiful blonde a second ago. "I'm not mean to anyone, but I won't sit by and let them hook you either. Being quiet has only led to my anxiety and others thinking they can bully me. I'm trying to change that." I yanked out my ear buds from my bag and popped one in. "Where the Wild Things Are" by Luke Combs plays in my ear.

With his arm secure on my shoulders and my arm around his waist, my gaze shifts back to the doors of doom. The idea of meeting new people makes my heart bustle. Maybe I'll get lucky and no one will try to talk to me. I squeeze my necklace with my free hand, praying the peace and fun I had with Nik will somehow morph from the necklace into my body. Maybe Princess Aurora's three good fairies could turn me into a dolphin and I could swim to the Mediterranean Sea and see Nik again.

Yeah, I know it won't happen, but dreaming gets me through the day.

Want to know what isn't a dream? Italy. Nik. Graduation. With my diploma in hand, I'll board a plane and find him.

In the meantime, I inhale a deep breath and slowly let it out.

"That's it, Kee. You got this." We joke and hassle each other, some-times we even yell and argue, mostly about the way Dad treats me, but it's times like this, I know he has my back and I have his. I grip my brother's shirt and he pulls me into his side a little more.

⚽†⚽†⚽

My bag strap rests on my shoulder, and my fingers grip the doorknob. The moment Principal Williams stops talking, I am out. The last thing I want is for someone to blame me for keeping them from what they're doing.

"I know your dad isn't happy that the soccer team is co-ed, but Maine has an entire Co-ed league for middle and high school Christian schools. None of the schools have enough students for traditional teams."

Co-ed? He can't be serious. That's what Dad gets for moving us to one of the top ten least populated states in the country. He's probably trying to discourage me from playing soccer. He expresses his frustration with my sport of choice ever since I started playing. I'll play until I can't walk just to show him he can't make me play a sport just because he wants me to. *Ugh.*

"Coach Bucci tells me that you're our ticket to a winning soccer season."

Great, more pressure.

"I doubt I'm essential to your success. Just an added bonus." I force a smile, hoping he'll let me leave, so I don't have to walk into class after the bell rings.

It'll be a miracle if these soccer players don't talk smack about me. Joining a team after the season has started can be detrimental if the players think I got special treatment. Now, I have to worry about the guys giving me a hard time if I take their playing time.

As I leave the office, jitters shake the already flitting butterflies in my stomach. I spot EJ casually leaning against the wall, surrounded by a coven of blood sucking vampires of the female variety, thirsty for breakfast, lunch, and dinner, and they've feasted their eyes on my brother. The guys in the group must be EJ's football teammates with their broad shoulders and loud, cocky presence.

If I was shopping for a boyfriend, which I'm not, I'd never date a football player. It doesn't matter anyway because even if I wanted a boyfriend, guys weren't interested in me like that. I'd always been one of the guys to hang around with, not go out with. That's okay. I'm not interested in dating anyway.

Yes, I'm trying to convince myself!

However, my heart stumbles down the hall as my eyes lock onto one of the guys in the group with his back to me. He stands at least six feet, probably taller, and he has broad, muscular shoulders. No doubt a football player. His fluffy hair screams for my fingers to run through it. Just then he whips his head back, getting the hair out of his eyes and my stomach quivers. I must be hungry because there's no way I'd be interested in someone by just seeing the back of them, even though everything about him is very impressive. My body hasn't reacted this way since Nik. *Ah, my first crush.* The way my heart holds onto him, *crush,* may not be a strong enough word.

I hate that I question everything. My mom refers to that as 'one of the unique qualities' I developed since returning to the states.

Maybe it's my anxiety flaring up, but the strong desire to join the group creates a fizzy, unsettling feeling in my stomach. EJ laughs at whatever the guy says, like they were long lost buddies.

How does he let people in so quickly? Why can't I do that? In a word, my dad. Fine, that's two words, but when someone lets you down and puts you down over and over again, you lose faith in humankind. That's where I am.

Nik's betrayal didn't help. I wrote him twenty letters before giving up. We'd promised to write to each other every week.

After arriving back in America, I kept up my end of the deal well beyond the humiliation stage, but he never did. He's probably dating some gorgeous Italian model and that's why he didn't write.

See what I mean? Just one of the guys. I wasn't even that important to Nik, or he would have written at least once, right?

I find myself staring at the group with longing eyes just as a trio of girls rounds the corner, almost barreling over me.

"Oh, excuse you." It's the blonde from the parking lot. Her tone drips with snarkiness. *Yup, she's the leader of this she-pack.*

When she follows my eyes to the group—rather, the guy I couldn't take my eyes off—she whips back around, demanding my attention. "Don't even think about it." Her acrylic nails splay across her low tummy as she grips her hips. "Most of them are taken and the tall one will be mine when I tell him. Not that he'd be interested in you anyway."

Don't look away. Girls like her smell fear and anxiety like a tracker dog. Breathe 1... 2... 3... My chest inflates a little more than I'd like. *Please don't let them notice.*

I catch my breath long enough to say, "I don't go after guys, they come to me." Thankfully, my feet have a mind of their own and lead me away just as the leader's jaw unhinges and her posse blows out exaggerated breaths, "Ugh." I think I heard one girl say, "That wasn't nice, Trish."

Note to self: Avoid "Trish" and her claws at all cost.

Looks like I've created my own *anti*-fanclub. EJ will be so proud when I tell him.

I pull my phone from my pocket, secure one earbud, and trudge through the hall. My Instagram feed calls me, so I scroll through while I listen to my self-proclaimed theme song—*Misfits* by Shinedown. I don't belong here like the song says, but it would be better if Nik and I were still on the same continent so we could be misfits together like we had been.

I don't need to look up to know that people are staring at me. I feel them. The sensation of a million centipedes crawling on my skin sends a shiver down my spine.

I never get to stay in one place long enough to make friends (just enemies). Apparently I've turned into an overachiever—I've never created enemies so quickly before. Hopefully everyone else pretends I'm not here.

3

MY LEG BOUNCES UNDER my desk. The teacher is rambling on about Hitler and Mussolini's Pact of Steel during World War II. I plead with my brain to focus on the subject, but it rebels. All I can think about is Keeley.

The imagined sight of her. So close, it sends a cold wave of dread washing over me, a stark reminder of the pain I thought I'd buried. What happened? If I hadn't forgotten her letter the day the authorities ripped me from my home, I might already have my answer. My leg bounces faster, not ready to deal with that either.

"Gotta watch out for those Italians, right Mrs. Weatherby?" Vinny interrupts, her sympathetic eyes meeting mine.

As captain of the soccer team, the guy thinks he's Mr. Universe. He has two things against me. His place on the soccer team isn't in danger that I know of, but he acts like I'm here to take him out.

Not the case.

Trish, the captain of the dance team, is second. The usual high school gossip spreads through the water fountains, carrying the news that she's claimed me as hers... Is that my fault? No, but it is my problem.

Dàtimi na pausa. Give me a break. I'm not interested in a girl like her.

That's not to say I won't use the rumor to my advantage and have a little fun with my teammate. "Yeah, we Sicilians tend to get everything we want." I flash a charming grin in his direction, hoping to twist the knife. Just. A little. More.

Turning toward the teacher, old enough to be my grandmother, I smile. "You were saying, Mrs. Weatherby."

A slight hue of pink rises to her cheeks as she returns to her lecture on World War II dictators.

Normally, I wouldn't have given Vinny the time of day, but talking with EJ this morning and his football buddies ignited a shot of adrenaline in my veins that hasn't slowed. The idea of Keeley being in this school has my nerve endings firing on all cylinders.

My emotions are on the brink of civil war. Let's be honest, she crushed my soul and it hasn't fully recovered. *Does it count if she doesn't know she did it?* I ask myself, hoping that is truly the case. My heart will completely disintegrate if I fall for her again and she moves, or my dad's situation changes and I have to return to Sicily.

She might only think of me as a friend. That possible realization slams against my chest harder than a center back, preventing me from scoring. Maybe it's better if I don't see her; don't get hooked again.

For me, I'll always be a Sicilian, so it's possible I'd be the one to leave. Speaking of leaves, (Yeah, I know we weren't, but my mind wanders when I'm nervous) they're starting to change color here and are as vibrant as Sicily's. The yellows, reds, and oranges are the same, but this place is missing the deep rust and ochre colors. The latter puts a picture of Keeley's hair in my mind. *No surprise there.* I used to love the feel of it when she'd rest her head on my shoulder as it cascaded down, tickling my bare arms.

As much as I love Sicily, I'd stay here if she asked me. I'm getting ahead of myself since I haven't even seen her yet. I can't imagine any of this will even matter since she only sent me one letter.

The locked door jiggles, pulling me from my musing. With threats against schools, all classroom doors are locked once classes start. I think teachers like that so kids can't sneak in late without them noticing.

"Please get the door, Nikolaus," Mrs. Weatherby snaps, her voice tight with barely suppressed irritation.

Students begin whispering, waiting to see who's on the other side. When I open the door, my fingers freeze on the knob, and my tongue waves, in ribbon fashion, back and forth trying to produce saliva. Without it, I am unable to speak.

She's only grown more beautiful. My heart thumps against my ribs, stirring up how much I've missed her.

Our eyes glue to one another. "Hi." *Seriously? I couldn't come up with something better than that?"*

Nope. Not when she is frowning and a wave of uncertainty crashes through me. Its sudden impact pounds me with such force it engulfs me in a vortex wall of water, leaving me gasping for air when the wave recedes, threatening to pull me out to sea with its mighty undertow, further away from the girl in front of me.

"Hi." Her expression changes to a confused state. That's a little better.

"Mr. Valentino, who's at the door?" Mrs. Weatherby's teacher voice jumps me, reminding me we're not alone.

I move to the side and wave Keeley through.

"How can I help you, Miss?"

Keeley hands the teacher her late slip. "I'm in this class."

"You're late." Mrs. Weatherby likes to intimidate students with her stern rules and voice. I find myself standing next to Keeley.

She points to the paper in Mrs. Weatherby's hand. "May I sit down?"

The teacher eyes Keeley up and down. "You may. Please don't make a habit of being late."

Keeley shakes her head and then pauses when her eyes capture something or someone in the back of the room. Trish. The dance captain glares back at Keeley, causing my anger to bubble to the surface. I gently cup Keeley's elbow, gaining her attention and nod my head toward the empty seat—conveniently right next to mine.

She doesn't pull away and embarrass me in front of the class, but her muscles tense and I know she's not happy with the contact, so I pull back.

Not a great start. Really? I hadn't noticed. Why does my brain want to point out the overly rough parts in my life? Because it hates me. That's the only logical reason... *Argh*!

Class drags on all the while I stare at Keeley. In my defense, she is in line with Mrs. Weatherby. I try to pay attention to the teacher's lecture, forcing my eyes to track her and my ears to hear her words, but the extra efforts are fruitless, no match for my brain, preparing what I'll say to Keeley. This goes without saying, but deserves recognition—Keeley is a million times better to look at.

Apparently, others notice my staring, because they laugh when Mrs. Weatherby assigns us as partners for the upcoming project. *Project?* What did I miss?

This could be a great way for us to rekindle our friendship.

Except, didn't I just say she would tear me to shreds if I let her back in? *Project or no project we can't work together,*

"That's not fair," Trish blurts out. "You've always let us pick our own partners."

In a school this small, the cliques are easy to find. Trish and her dance team <u>think</u> they run the school. That might have something to do with her father being headmaster and her mother holds the Treasurer position on the board.

Working with Keeley, it would be difficult to not fall right back into the same place we were in Italy. My traitorous heart thinks it's a great idea, but my brain is more logical. Our dad's told us before that they didn't want us hanging out together. I can't imagine anything has changed.

But working with Trish would be torture. *She's a picciotta scarsa.* Calling her a mean girl doesn't truly paint the exact picture (she's worse), but you get the point.

I glance over at Keeley. Either way, I am going to lose. If I agree to work with Keeley, I'll lose my heart. If I allow Trish to worm her way into working with me, I'll lose my mind.

She's your best friend, one you have more than friendly feelings for, whether you admit it or not. Not working with her isn't going to change reality. Very logical thinking; thank you brain.

I see the way some of the guys are ogling Keeley. I can't have her working closely with them, they'll try to take advantage of her. They all need lessons in how to treat women. *Don't be stupid, your heart hasn't healed from Keeley ditching you and ignoring your letters.* My mischievous side has two valid points.

"Trish, I appreciate your input, but I've decided I'm making the partner choices this time." Mrs. Weatherby glances in my direction.

The sight of Keeley's smile eases my tension, a gentle balm to my frayed nerves.

"Sounds good. Whatever you say, Mrs. Weatherby." *Who just said that?* No, no, I heard my own voice, but those were not the words my brain intended to say. Even Keeley looks a little shocked at my willingness.

Trust me, no one is more shocked than me.

Luckily, the teacher moves on to assign the next students, giving my brain a chance to catch up with my mouth's betrayal.

For the last few minutes of class, I pay no attention to the other groups. Instead, my mind gravitates back to Keeley. She seems different. Not necessarily in a bad way, but distant or sad, maybe both. For all the past anger, an equal amount of concern bubbles to the surface.

What has she been through the past couple of years? When she leaves, will she avoid me again? Can we return to being friends? Will we ever be more?

I feel like I'm drowning in uncertainty as the unanswered questions gnaw at me. A bitter resentment, clashing with my desire to jump all in, rises in my throat with each unanswered question.

4

Keeley

REALIZATION HITS ME AS I make my way through the hallway—Nik isn't the same boy I left behind two years ago. Yet he's undeniably the guy I spotted with EJ this morning. We've both grown since the last day in Italy, but we're still close enough so kissing won't strain his neck. Not much, anyway.

Whoa, pump the brakes on the smooching. The mad voice from some-where within the abyss of my mind decides that now is the right time to remind me that Nik ghosted me and is apparently Trish's property. I don't fight the urge to roll my eyes.

EJ is dead meat when I get to our lockers. I would have told him if he was about to reunite with his long-lost crush.

And just like that, my mind is back on Nik. *Ooh and those muscles.* I could almost hear the fun side of my brain laughing and cheering for a sweet reunion with him.

Describing Nik's muscles is easy. The ones he had two years ago had babies and they are now working on having babies of their own.

It was hard enough to concentrate with Mrs. Weatherby going on and on about dead dictators from almost a hundred years ago, but when Nik crossed his arms over his chest and his veins popped... *Wow!* Some might not find that attractive. Good, more for me because my insides are still melting.

Nik still has mesmerizing blue eyes and brown fluffy hair that might be a little more wavy than before. I should still be mad that he never wrote to me, and believe me, I am, but...

I pick up my speed as the hallway in front of me clears, grateful for the breeze I get from students walking the other direction.

When I reach my locker, EJ is waiting for me. "Hey, do you know who goes to school here?"

Really? That's how he's going to play this. I grip his arm and jump up and down. "Yes, Selena Gomez! She is the best, isn't she?"

"Yeah. Wait! Are you for real?"

I laugh and roll my eyes as I press my palm against his arm, pushing him out of the way. He knows.

"Are you mad I didn't tell you?"

Mad? *No. More like disappointed or upset.* "I would have liked to prepare myself."

"Right. Your anxiety would have landed you in the nurse's office, not with Nik."

He's right again. *Darn him!* I slam my door and we walk to the locker room.

That's interesting though—my anxiety didn't flare at all with Nik around. I only received a diagnosis a year and a half ago. *Hmmm, Maybe Mom was right about this coming on when we returned.*

"We were partnered up for a project in US History. Dad won't like that." If anyone knows how my dad feels, it's EJ. They are like two college buddies talking football around the clock. Dad never has time to do any of my hobbies with me, but he'll do anything EJ asks. *Whatever.* I inhale and exhale a humongous breath.

He shrugged. "Do it at Nik's."

Well, well. My brows raise, and he bumps my shoulder.

"He already hurt you once. You better not let him back in." He shook his fist in the air. A burst of unrestrained laughter spills from my lips, chasing away my brother's weak attempt at intimidation.

His eyes glare at me. They look eerily similar to a rabid animal, ready to pounce. *Maybe he's serious.* If only he was there to protect me last night when Dad cornered me after dinner.

"Take off those stupid headphones," he barked as he entered my room.

I hesitated for a second. Just long enough for my heart to thump against my ribs. I slid them off my head and onto my bed.

"Who are you listening to?"

"One Direction."

He sighs and pitches his voice a few octaves higher. "You need better taste in music."

"What did you want?"

"Don't you think for a second your mother will believe you over me. Remember, I put a roof over your head and food in your mouth. Stop being ungrateful.

I didn't lie. He ignored me every time I asked him a question, but when my mother entered the room, he asked me what I had for homework. Like he cares. He's never helped me with my work once. He just wanted to sound good in front of Mom. He's trying to turn Mom against me.

I reached for my headphones. Just holding them will help me breathe better. He swiped them from my grip. "I'll bust these stupid things if you don't pay attention to me."

Anger ran through my veins, pulsing through my blood. He's such a jerk!

"Where's your God now?"

"Kee, are you okay?" EJ grips my trembling hand, yanking me back to the present.

I nod and take a deep breath. The look on his face says he doesn't believe I am, but neither of us speaks as we make our way through the gym.

That gives my mind plenty of time to focus on Nik. The frown on his face at the end of class worries me. What if he flakes his responsibility in this project like when he failed to write to me? Maybe he doesn't have the desire to be friends anymore?

"Football gets out at four. Is soccer the same?" EJ intrudes on my anxious thoughts. I guess I should thank him. They were headed down a long windy road I've visited before that leads nowhere.

I nod. "Yup. Meet at Etna, okay?" He agrees and pulls open the locker room door and disappears.

No judging. Yes, I named my Volkswagen Tiguan, Etna. That's my favorite place on Earth, thanks to Nik.

The sound of teenaged boys shouting over slamming lockers wafts into the gym. I wonder if Nik is in there already.

A memory of playing soccer with him in Italy pops into my head. After too many minutes staring at the boys' locker room door, daydreaming of days gone by, my Italian Dreamboat appears.

"You must be thinking about me with a smile like that."

"Well, if it isn't Mr. I'm full of myself." He really isn't, but he caught me off guard, so I had to say something.

"Your smile. It's *bedda*."

I can't tell exactly what color my cheeks are, but heat rushes up my neck and into my face. It would happen to any girl if Nik called her beautiful in Sicilian. *Italians are so romantic.*

"Don't start with that Sicilian nonsense."

He nudges me with his shoulder before he crosses his arms, and his bulging veins steal my attention again. "Come on, that's not what you say."

Whenever he called me beautiful, I returned the compliment once he taught me the Sicilian word for a beautiful male. *When I get the nerve, I'll have him teach me some new words to describe him.*

Nik laughs as he bends his knees and dips his head until his eyes capture mine. "Like what you see?"

Drat. He caught me. I roll my eyes and shove his arm. He doesn't budge. "You are *beddu.*" The urge to squeeze his arm fills my fingers.

"There's my girl." His expression changes; it's one akin to shock, and he runs his hand through his hair. Was it normal to be jealous of someone else's hand? *Probably not.*

My heart speeds up, wondering if his sheepish expression and words mean something more, or if being this close to him is too much for me. *We're just friends.* I remind myself.

"Listen, I'm still mad at you. It's not fair to play the nice guy now."

"*Mi scusassi?*"

"Yes, excuse you. I wrote so many letters, but you never wrote me back."

"You never showed."

My stomach drops, as we stare at each other. The pain in his eyes nearly tears me in half. Before I can get my next words out, Coach Bucci appears.

"Valentino, James, what are you waiting for? Get changed and meet us on the field."

"Yes, Coach," we replied in unison.

"This isn't over." His deep voice sends a shiver down my spine. No one needs to sound <u>that</u> dreamy.

I nod and give him the best smile I can as I disappear into the locker room.

It's been hard being away from Nik all these years, but worse, seeing him hurt. I hope this doesn't ruin our chance at being friends again.

Soccer practice flew by in a blur. Spoiler alert—no one except for Nik likes me intruding on their team. Now I'm on my bed working on homework.

Attempting to work is more accurate. My fleeting thoughts keep returning to practice.

If Princess Aurora is sweet and kind, my new teammate named Aurora is Maleficent. Coach Bucci asked her to warm up with me, yet she refused to acknowledge me at all.

Beryl, the girl captain, is the Trish of the soccer team. She must eat snarky comments for breakfast and use them as weapons throughout the day.

These girls are child's play compared to my last school, but it doesn't make them any less pesky. Every girl except for Aurora and Beryl hit on Nik the entire time. *I wonder if I'm still the only one allowed to call him Nik?* My eyes pool with tears, realizing I don't know this Nik.

Dad and EJ's voices penetrate through my closed door, pulling me back to my untouched homework. They must be debating football stats or players—something that keeps them close and me on the outside.

My mind drifts back to Nik. I wonder what he's doing right now? If only I would have asked for his number, I could text him. Ha! Imagine if he didn't respond to me.

I didn't get a chance to see him after practice, but Vinny, the boy captain, strutted over to me like a peacock, with his pretty boy face and perfectly gelled hair after a shower. "If you need anything, let me know." He shook my hand and dragged his fingertips across my palm as he released.

"Uh, hi," I'd said and pulled my hand back.

Hours later, I'm still wondering what the heck is wrong with him.

You know, he had the audacity to smirk at me and say, *"Oh, you're one of those girls who plays hard to get."*

For the record, no, I don't play anything. Even if Vinny outlasted every other guy on Earth, I would never, ever date the likes of him.

Okay, so back to a better topic. Nik. Besides his physical changes, he seems different—his smile and eyes are hard. I know his dad could be a challenge. It's doubtful it got any better. But his mom. Oh, I love his mom, Rachel. She is the sweetest woman ever.

I grab my pillow and pull it to my chest, as an exciting thought rushes through my body. If Nik's dad broke cultural norms by marrying an American, Nik might do the same. Yes, I still might have a chance. I kick my legs in the air and nearly suffocate myself with my pillow, muffling my scream.

I wonder if I could call Rachel? Our moms are friends or were friends. Come to think of it, I haven't noticed my mom talking about Rachel for a while now. I hope they didn't have a falling out, and that's why Nik didn't write to me. *Nah, I can't blame our moms' friendship for Nik not wanting to keep in contact.*

A knock at my door startles me. "Come in."

"Hey, sis, dinner's ready."

I stand, grab my brother's arm, pull him into my room, and shut the door.

"Geez. What's the deal?"

My shoulders shrug and I give him a sheepish look. "What did you and Nik talk about?"

A slow smirk stretches across my brother's lips, a mischievous glint in his eyes. He knows I would give just about anything for answers.

"I'll tell you if I can drive Etna." He raised his brows, waiting for my response.

My brother's truck is in the shop, getting fixed from his fender bender. Why would I let him drive mine? *Because I want answers.*

"Give me the deets," I sigh and he smiles.

"There's a party..."

Not the deets I meant.

"A party?" *Of course, I wasn't invited.*

"...you can come, too, if you want."

Gee, thanks for the secondary invite. To be fair, I haven't made an attempt to be friends with anyone since we left Italy. It's too hard to know who's being a real friend. I've found it easier to focus on school and soccer, nothing else.

"You know I don't—"

"Nik will be there."

I freeze. That makes all the difference. "Maybe."

Just then Dad bellows up the stairs, "Come on, kids, dinner is getting cold."

I roll my eyes, feeling annoyed that he interrupted something important to me again.

"Give him a break, would ya?"

Of course, EJ takes his side. I never thought there'd come a day when I'd have to be careful about what I say or do around my brother.

"You need to tell me what Nik said," I grab his arm before he can run off.

"He asked me not to tell you."

My heart sinks. Yup, he has a girlfriend, or worse another best friend...

He can have a girlfriend, whatever, that's fine. But we made a promise, I'll be his best friend until the day I die. I can't figure out what emotion is on my face, but EJ gives me a hug.

Dad calls again, and EJ squeezes me tight before leaving my room.

I hate feeling alone, but I do because no one understands me. Nik used to...

There's only one way to find out if he still does.

5

THIS ISN'T THE WORST school I've been to, but I'm exhausted. Though childish, Trish's dirty looks and knocking my books over were elementary pranks. Besides, every time Trish acted nasty, Nik showed up like my own personal hero and swept me away.

It's obvious why every girl drools over him. If I wasn't trying to revitalize our best friend status...

The thought jars me back to the present where Dad and EJ are probably still talking about football. I can't wait until dinner is over so I can go back to my room.

Dad stuffed a few chips into his mouth. "You're going, right?"

"No," I say with a flat tone, not knowing where I just declined to go, but if Dad wants me to go...

"If she doesn't want to go, we need to respect her wishes," my mom says diplomatically.

Please, someone tell me where I'm <u>not</u> going.

Dad gulps his soda and sets his glass on the table. "The only way to make friends is to put yourself out there. Go have fun."

Why? So you can tell me that I need to learn how to pick better friends. No, thank you.

I kept my eyes closed, making sure I didn't roll them, or I'd hear about that for twenty minutes and still get a lecture about not wanting to go wherever he's trying to force me.

Dad tapped the table with his pointer finger, bringing my attention back to him. I slid one side of my headphones off my ear to hear him. "This will not be like Ohio. For a week you've gone to school, soccer, and spent the rest of your time in your room. Not happening here. Isn't that Nikolaus boy from Italy on your soccer team?"

How does he know that?

"Why aren't you hanging out with him? Your mother told me you two were inseparable in Italy."

Something is sus. "You wouldn't let us. Remember, you *borrowed*"—I use air quotes and sarcasm to emphasize the word—"my Vespa so I couldn't see him on the final day there."

"Yup, always accusing me of doing things that I don't."

Anger, like a riptide, rushes through me. I'm tired of him making himself look good in front of Mom and EJ when he is calculating.

"I'm sure you also remember that he didn't respond to any of the letters I sent him. Why do you want me to go through that again?" I answer silently for him—because you don't like me.

Mom put a hand on my forearm. "I'm sure that's not what Dad wants." She glares at him. We all know that look—the one where mom is telling Dad to fix it, or else.

Dad's eyes and tone soften when he says, "I'm trying to right my wrongs. It's been a long time. Please forgive me for whatever I did, Keeley."

Hogwash! This is what he does. He's trying to get me to let my guard down so he can get close to me. Why would I want to be near him when he tells me everything I do and think is wrong?

"Why aren't you pressuring EJ to go?"

"Because I'm talking to you." I hate when he says that. In adult language, that means: *I don't have a good answer for you because I'm wrong, but I get to make you do what I want because I'm the parent.*

I go with a safe answer. Dad would never want anything to interfere with soccer. "I have a game on Monday. I should rest up and be ready for that."

He clears his throat and glares at me probably hoping I change my mind. I won't.

I can see it in his eyes; I'm going to win this one. Feigning the need to be ready for soccer always gets me out of things.

"That's fine for this week, but starting next week, I want you to go," Dad insists.

I don't agree since I still don't know what he's talking about, but Dad will consider this a done deal because he *said so.* Maybe by next week, I'll want to go and then it will be a non-issue.

"Thank you. May I be excused, please?"

Dad nods. "Take your plate to the sink first."

I get halfway down the hallway, already dreaming about collapsing on my bed before dad stops me.

"Please give your keys to EJ; he's going to youth group tonight. Since you aren't going anywhere, he'll take the Volkswagen.

Argh! First, is it that difficult to call her Etna? For him, yes. Why? He said it was stupid to name a car, especially after a volcano. *"You'll be sorry if it blows up like a volcano one day."* His comment rushes back. That wasn't funny then and it's not funny now, but Dad laughed like his life depended on it. *Whatever.* Second, how can he just lend my car out to EJ and why didn't EJ ask me? *Because he knew I'd say no.*

I still haven't responded to my dad and EJ is staring down at his plate when my phone vibrates in my pocket. The moment I pull it out, I feel flush reading the preview banner with an unknown number.

Unknown: Keeley. It's Nik.

Keeley: What's up

I store his name in my phone.

Italian Dreamboat: U coming 2 youth group

EJ gave me your number. I hope that's okay

Why didn't he ask me for my number? There's nothing worse than people doing things behind my back.

Is Nik asking because he wants me to go? Maybe I should put myself out there; reunite with him. Find out if there's anything more than friendship between us.

Keeley: R U?

Italian Dreamboat: Yeah

When I arrived here a week ago, I thought it would be the worst place Dad had ever dragged us to, but Nik alone makes this place more appealing by the minute.

I guess it won't kill me to go. "What time are we leaving EJ?"

"It starts at seven," he says, sounding equal parts shocked and relieved.

After showering, I wait while EJ gets ready. My mind drifts to a far-off place, and doubt slams into me like a barge. What if Nik is just playing a sick game on me? My mom says that our experiences shape us. No wonder I don't trust people. Something about this whole situation just doesn't feel right, but I can't put my finger on it.

Why didn't Nik ask me for my number himself? But more importantly, why is Dad encouraging me to hang out with Nik?

An hour later, EJ and I are walking into school. "Come on, Kee, don't be upset. The guy asked. What was I supposed to do?"

"It's simple you open your mouth and say, 'If you want Keeley's number, ask her.'"

"I'm sorry. But I have to admit, you're very confusing." I tug on his arm, preventing him from moving any further. I hope the glare I'm giving him is as fierce as it feels.

"Explain yourself."

He shakes his head and shifts from one foot to the other. What doesn't he want to tell me? "Fine. You've been miserable since we left Italy. For a week you've had Nik back in your life and you're still miserable."

Miserable? *No.* On guard? *Maybe. Probably.* Okay, fine. *Yes.*

"There are too many unanswered questions and I don't want to play the fool again."

EJ clutches both my shoulders. "You just said you have unanswered questions, so stop assuming he played you. The way he looks at you, let's just say, I know that look and I'll kill him this time if he hurts you again...in any way."

There's the EJ I know. He's a little scary and super sweet. "Thanks, Bro. Let's get this over with." He stares at me. "I mean, let's go see what this is all about."

"Better."

After a Bible lesson and enough glares from Trish and her posse to last a lifetime, I think it's over.

Finally.

Then the two couples who run the group divide the teens in half for a friendly competition of dodgeball.

Nik and I end up on Brent and his wife, Andrea's, team. Even after one lesson, I can tell these two people are God-fearing people. Andrea shared her story of love and loss. I don't know what I'd do if I lost my parents in a car accident, that also took away my ability to walk.

After multiple surgeries, she is now mobile. She has a walker and they keep her wheelchair in their truck for emergencies, but it's been almost two years and she keeps improving. Unfortunately, she won't be of any help to us in this game because she's pregnant and Brent is treating her like she's glass.

Awwwww. Men like that only exist in books and movies, and they wonder why romance novels generate the most sales. Women need good men. If men read these books, maybe women wouldn't need to escape to a romantic world so often. Just a thought, but I'm sure I'm too young to know anything. At least, that's what my dad says.

Joe and Donna are talking with their team. I should be paying attention to Brent's directions, but the girl who hangs with Trish is currently snuggled up to my brother. Anyway, my head isn't in the game and I get eliminated quickly. These couples are ultimate competitors, so watching them alone is interesting. Within a minute, Nik is sitting next to me on the bleacher. I won't accuse him of botching the play, but I think he dropped the ball on purpose.

He's just as competitive as I am, so that's probably the hopeless romantic within making myself feel better.

His chest is heaving and his sparkling eyes are pinned on me. I should feel flattered, but with Trish's laser beam stares, all I can do is disintegrate. I feel trapped and uncomfortable, My betraying watch says it's not time to leave.

"Have you dated a lot since we've last seen each other?"

WHAT?! The question fell out of my mouth without any chance of me stopping it. To make matters worse, he must know how nervous I am to hear his answer because he rests his hand on my shoulder. He used to do that all the time when I got upset with my dad and that always worked. Until now.

At the moment, my shoulder is burning like his hand is molten lava from Mount Etna herself.

This is so embarrassing.

I dip my head to prevent him from seeing what I imagine are deep red, possibly crimson, cheeks. "I'm sorry. I don't know why I asked that. It's none of my business and I don't—"

He grins, stopping my mouth from further humiliation. *Thank you.*

His gaze latches onto me like a leech to the limb of an overzealous swimmer.

No, I'm not calling him a leech, unless leeches are now six feet tall, broad-shouldered specimens of yumminess.

If he's waiting me out to see how long before my heart stops or my lungs burst, it won't be much longer.

Sadly, he still hasn't answered. Maybe he is trying to be nice, not wanting me to cry in front of these new people.

"Hey, me a-mor-ay," Trish glides past us, making flirty eyes at Nik and trying, but failing her best attempt at the Sicilian dialect. "Nik, feel free to join us over here where the company isn't so blah." Trish blows him a kiss as she sashays past.

"It's Nikolaus and no, thanks. I'm happy where I am."

My inner self cheers. Even if I am not responsible for him being happy, I'm happy he doesn't follow her.

Everyone around us is chatting amongst themselves. When did all these people arrive? I look around dumbfounded that there are only three people left in the entire game: two on Nik and my team and one on the other.

Seconds later, Nik leans closer, torturing me with his clean, ocean scent. The heat from his mouth fans my cheek when he says low and husky, "I haven't dated anyone, but I think that needs to change."

Oh, my 'Lanta! Yes, Full House was the first show my mom let me watch that wasn't a cartoon or the Brady Bunch and I stole DJ's line, but there isn't another one as fitting.

Did he just say he hasn't dated anyone? *Yes, he did. EEEEK!*

Did he say things will change now that I am here? *No!*

He said he wanted to date. Maybe he was talking about dating Trish? But I don't think so based on the way he glared at her in American History class and the way he shut her down a few moments ago. Why do I have to second guess everything?

Anyway, the dodgeball game is over. EJ won. *Surprise, surprise.*

"Did you see that, sis? I not only out lasted you, but I took the whole game."

Normally, I'd have some comeback, even challenge him to a rematch, but not right now. The heat radiating from Nik's body next to me feels like a sauna.

"I have to…" EJ and Nik stare at me, waiting for me to finish making up something I have to go do.

I've got nothing.

"Yeah, I've got to go. EJ, I'll meet you at Etna," I say with the steadiest tone I can manage before I sprang from the bleachers, forcing myself to walk and not bolt from the gym.

An hour later, I am washed up and ready for bed. I tap my playlist and punch my pillow a few times, hoping to release the worry and doubt building inside of me. Why'd I just leave? I should have asked Nik what he meant, but I chickened out. As I listen to my music, I'm being pulled further and further into the abyss of uncertainty, devoid of sleep.

I try scrolling Instagram, my eyes still wide. When my playlist repeats the first song, I swipe my phone off its stand—one thirty. Great. I'll be trash for tomorrow's practice if I don't get to sleep now.

Keeley's heart flutters when the text banner at the bottom of her screen appears.

Italian Dreamboat: I didn't wake you did I

Keeley: No

Can't sleep

Wbu?

Italian Dreamboat: Me either

I'm bored

Keeley: Gee, thanks

Italian Dreamboat: It's not like that

Ur emotional

Keeley: FR?

Italian Dreamboat: Yeah. I've seen you cry

Keeley: You mean the time you had me walk on the black sand near Etna. That stuff is hot

Italian Dreamboat: See UR emotional

Keeley: I'll be sure to repay the favor

Italian Dreamboat: You already did when you kicked me with the ball. I'll be lucky to have kids one day

Keeley: I apologized

Wuss

Italian Dreamboat: Don't you know that hurts

Keeley: Oh, but my feet didn't

Italian Dreamboat: Not as bad

Keeley: Whatever! They burned for a week

Italian Dreamboat: I fell over

Keeley: So dramatic

I grin, realizing how much I missed teasing Nik.

Italian Dreamboat: Ur the only one still allowed to call me Nik

I noticed he corrected Trish, but didn't want to get my hopes up that it meant something. I don't have words, so I send a smiling emoji.

Italian Dreamboat: Why'd you run off?

Keeley: I wasn't feeling right

Not a lie. Whenever he's close my body temperature rises well beyond healthy limits.

Italian Dreamboat: Are you better now?

Surface level? Sure. Deep down. Not even close.

Keeley: I should get some sleep.

My heavy eyelids threatened to shut out the world.

Italian Dreamboat: Yeah, I don't want to embarrass u at practice tomorrow

Keeley: Now I can laugh myself to sleep

Goodnight, Nik

Italian Dreamboat: Night, Keeley

My face hurts from smiling, and my hollowed out stomach is fluttering. I'd never expected to have Nik back in my life. I'm glad Dad got transferred here. I might not be saying that come winter, but I'm feeling warm enough right now. Sadly, I know how quickly things can change.

6

I WISH I COULD make Keeley's transition to this school easier. There hasn't been a time since I arrived in America that I felt more alive than I do when Keeley is around.

Our closeness is affecting her as much as it is me. I can see it, even if she won't admit it. At Saturday's practice Beryl had every girl giving Keeley attitude or keeping the ball from her. Coach Bucci didn't say a word. Not even when Vinny took her ball and taunted her with expletives.

"Stop flexing, Vinny, and play. Does Keeley's superiority frighten you?" Nik's words sparked the team, who responded with a round of "Oooohs," their voices a mixture of excitement and surprise.

Coach did, however, threaten to bench me when I shoved Vinny to the ground. Shock split Keeley's face and she placed her hands on my abs, preventing me from going after him more. *'He's not worth it.'* My body is still lit up with awareness from her touch.

I'm waiting in my car this morning, searching the lot for her little SUV—sweet Etna. Her words continue to race through my mind again.

She's right; he's not worth it, but Keeley's worth everything. I'll fight for her and protect her from anyone.

An unknown number rings my phone as I make my way into the school. I reject the call.

I lean against the entry way across from Keeley's locker and my phone rings again, the same unknown number. It's 7:30 in the morning, who could be calling?

I scan the hallway; still no Keeley. Swiping my finger across the screen, I whisper, "Hello?"

"Son."

"Dad, are you okay? Did you get out?"

He laughs. "Not yet. Give Bruni some time."

"It's been over a year." I don't say the rest of my thoughts—that he must be guilty if he hasn't been released yet. At the last update, he has five counts on his head, each punishable up to twenty years in prison. He'll never get out.

"I don't have long, but I wanted to check in with you. Everything going okay? Anything new I should know about?"

How did he always know when to check up on me? Yes, I said *up*. He's not concerned with checking in, like he says. He's making sure I'm following his orders. I've been instructed to get an education, and scout for a place where he can establish his business in America. This is very hard to do since I don't know *exactly* what he does. Everything is a need-to-know basis and I'm not in the know. I've come to the conclusion that I don't ever want to be *in the know*.

It's been years of him telling me this, so I am used to it, but today, I am eager to talk to Keeley and don't want to deal with any of my dad's *accidenti*. That's the closest Sicilian word for "crap" in English.

"My grandparents take good care of me here." I wonder briefly if he'll have a rude comment about them. There hasn't been any love loss between them my entire life.

"No doubt the money I send helps."

There it is. *Right, Dad, since everything is always about you!* Anger bubbles to the surface. If I want to have a clear mind to talk with Keeley, I need to go. Now.

"You're staying true to yourself, si?

The other order I'm expected to follow is to stay Sicilian. That's a challenge being in America with no one else who speaks my language. Though, now that Keeley's back in my life, maybe we could go back to speaking with each other in Sicilian. Even if I don't want to be part of the business, I don't want to lose my heritage.

"Yes, I need to go, Dad."

"Wait a minute."

I jam my hand under the arm holding my phone, hoping the little bit of movement will disconnect the call. No such luck.

"There will be multiple packages sent to your grandparents' address over the next few days. Sal will text you the address you need to deliver them to. Do not open the packages." Dad pauses. I remember his words the last time I delivered a package—'the less you know the better'—that was the day I missed seeing Keeley and telling her my feelings. Talk about regret.

I see Keeley and EJ walking this way. "I'm not doing anything with any of your packages. I have to go, arrivederci."

"Nikolaus!" His father's sharp voice prevents him from hanging up. "You don't do this and your reunion with Keeley will be even shorter than you can imagine."

My body freezes, only an icy ribbon of dread shooting down my spine brings my brain back to the conversation. "What are you talking about?"

Silence.

"Dad!" I whisper yell into my phone, but he's gone.

Instinctively, my fingers run through my hair. A minute ago, I'd say it was to look good for Keeley, now it's my nerves. *Focus on impressing Keeley. You can protect her from whatever Dad was hinting at.* I readjust the strap of my backpack and lean on the wall again. That's how I was the first time Keeley told me I was hot. I still blush remembering her explaining to me what being hot was. She became so shy after that.

She still hasn't seen me. Her and EJ are in a heated discussion. The halls are filling fast and Trish and her friends are headed this way. I'll do anything to avoid them.

My next move, however, has nothing to do with avoiding the mean girls and everything to do with rebuilding my relationship with Keeley.

"Buongiorno," My arm has more confidence than me as it wraps around Keeley's shoulders. Her smile is the perfect reward.

"Good morning, Nik."

"Come on, please tell me you didn't lose your Sicilian tongue. We can form our own group." My eyes darted to EJ for a second, but then back on Keeley. "It would be cool for the three of us to say things that keep others guessing, right?"

Keeley's eyes light up and I can tell she's considering what I said.

"Yeah, maybe."

Her bright smile told me she would play along with me when the time came.

"Hey, Nik, maybe you can settle the debate Keeley and I are having?"

"I'll try. Family stuff is hard."

EJ waved his hands. "Nope. This will be easy."

"For reasons you don't need to know, Keeley said I could use her..." he smirks ..."Etna to go to the party next week. But now, she's decided—"

"—You convinced me." My head turned toward Keeley, interrupting her brother.

"Semantics. She's decided to go to the party and she wants me to bring her."

My eyes never make their way back to EJ. Keeley's big green eyes remind me of the Mediterranean—usually calm and peaceful unless things are stirring within. Unsettling energy is brewing beneath her surface for sure.

What am I missing? After Keeley taught me the basics of the English language, my dad sent me to a private school to learn the language. I graduated from that school as the most fluent English speaker, but right now, trying to figure out their issue, I feel like a level I English Language Learner.

A surge of joy, warm and bright, fills my chest, knowing our time together explains that name. That and Keeley's slightly pink cheeks..

"Why can't you drive and she rides with you?" I shrug, feeling like I solved their issue, which never should have been a problem.

"I'm bringing a date."

Ah. That makes sense. My heart soars, realizing I have their answer.

"Since you promised him he could use your car, why don't I take you?"

Her shoulders tense. No, I still haven't removed my arm and she hasn't moved away, so I let it ride. But now, the palm of said hand slowly grazes her upper back as I pull away feeling horrible for making her uncomfortable and equally wishing my chest didn't ache as if my heart had just stopped beating.

Concern waves through my mind. *Is it me?* Keeley never worried about being alone with me before. Maybe she's not as interested in me as I am.

"Remember, we're friends. It's okay if we go together." I'm not sure my words help when Keeley winces, but EJ is ecstatic.

"That's a brilliant idea," EJ exclaims.

Keeley tugs on the hem of her shirt. *Why is she so nervous around me?*

"Sure," Keeley finally speaks. "What about Dad?"

The three of us are quiet for a moment.

"He still hates me, huh?"

Ej rests his hand on Keeley's open locker door. "I don't know what his deal is with you." Her brother's eyes lit up. "I could always drop you off with Nikolaus somewhere and then pick up my date?"

Keeley will never go for this. She always follows the rules.

"Works for me." She shrugs.

I guess she's changed. *Hopefully not too much.*

EJ doesn't wait to finalize plans before he runs down the hall, no doubt to ask someone to the party.

Fine with me.

"Are you sure you're okay with this?" I ask, leaning my shoulder against the lockers.

Her smile probably has everything to do with the lean and not my question, but I'll take it.

She finishes packing her bag with what she needs for class and slams the door shut.

"Are you okay with it? Don't feel like you have to babysit me. I probably won't go to the party anyway. I was just giving EJ a hard time."

Nah. She can't fool me.

I reach for her bag. "Let me."

I love the way a blush rises to her cheeks, like a long awaited sunrise.

"Where's your first class?" I ask, making my intention clear. I am walking her there personally.

She points toward the labs, and dips her head as she tucks a piece of hair behind her ear. With the easier access, I lean closer and whisper, "Do I make you nervous?"

Her head snaps up, her long hair, a furious whip, misses my face by a few centimeters. The delicate scent of orchids surrounding her brings me back to the first time I picked her a wild orchid by Mount Etna. She said it was the first time a guy had ever given her a flower and that was the first of her confessions. Heat swirls its way through my body.

We weave around a group of underclassmen taking up half the hallway.

"What? No. Why would you make me nervous?"

I smirk and shrug off her response not wanting to embarrass her. Because I like to punish myself, I lean in and smell her hair. Her body visibility shivers. *Yeah, I'm getting to her.* "What is that smell?"

She presses me away and I reluctantly move back into my own space. "It's an orchid shampoo I found on Amazon."

"Any particular reason you're buying shampoo from Amazon when you have stores two minutes away?"

A triumphant grin spread across my face. Soon, her admission will confirm my suspicions that it has to do with the flowers I gave her.

"It's cheaper," she barks and looks away quickly. I start laughing, knowing the truth. At least I *think* I *know* the truth.

"I've missed this," I start to say as she stops outside the Bio Lab. *I'm not ready to leave her.*

Her eyes are focused on the floor. I lift her chin with my finger. The allure of her lips is irresistible to me. Without my permission, my body leans close and I rest my palm on the wall behind her. My free hand moves to her cheek, hoping she doesn't flinch or move away. Success. *Yes!* No longer am I a scared fourteen year old boy unable to tell Keeley how much I like her. I'm not willing to let this girl escape from my life again.

Keeley places her palm on my chest, creating space between us. Her breath hitches. I chuckle, amused at how I affect her. Thankfully, she doesn't notice my pulse racing.

"We have a lot to talk about."

She's not wrong, but the rejection still stings.

"I know. Lunch today? I was hoping we could meet up and talk."

"Sure." Her hand is still on my chest, mine on her cheek. I lean in quickly kissing her on the top of the head.

"Until then."

"Ni videmu," Keeley says so low I would have missed it if my feet hadn't been rejecting the order to move.

She does remember my language. Cue the violins. I bop her on the nose as I say the English translation nice and low, "I will see you."

As I walk away, I look over my shoulder and see that she hasn't gone into class yet. Today is going to be a good day.

7

"TODAY HAS BEEN THE worst day of my life, and it's not even lunchtime," I grumble, staring down at my detention slip. To clarify, when Nik kissed my head, it was enough to make my skin spark like faulty electrical wiring. But then I entered Bio Lab and those wires lost connection.

With my eyes closed and my fist clenching the paper, I recall.

"I don't suppose this seat is taken," Trish's syrupy sweet voice makes me cringe. She has the audacity to sit next to me, ignoring the empty seats available. Before I can recall my brother's advice about being more friendly, Trish's claws come out. "I've been after Nikolaus since he arrived and there's no way someone like you is going to come along and steal him from me."

Yes, she said, 'Someone like you' as if I was beneath the lowest social class level.

"Listen, I've known Nik for years. If he was interested in you, would he have kissed me when he carried my bag and walked me to this class?" I

raise my brows, emphasizing not only my question, but the implication behind Nik and me being more than friends. She doesn't need to know all the details.

I can't lie. Her pout, though annoying, brings me satisfaction. "Why don't you do yourself a favor? Leave me alone." I move to a vacant seat.

She huffs. I imagine no one has ever talked to her that way before. The exaggerated noise captures the teacher's attention, and Mr. Lee gives me detention for moving my seat.

A slamming locker jolts me back to the present. I pull the office door open and enter Principal Williams's space to explain what happened since Mr. Lee wouldn't listen to my side of the situation. No surprise there. Adults always think they are right. When Mr. Williams found out the student is Trish Marsden, you would have thought I told him aliens were invading the cafeteria.

"I'm sorry, Keeley, there's nothing I can do."

"Excuse me. You're going to allow this girl to intimidate you? You can dismiss this, or explain to Mr. Lee what happened and have him rip up the slip."

When he still refuses, I find Coach Bucci. "Keeley, I know you've been to a lot of schools, but this one operates a little differently than most."

Tell me something I don't know. Coming here was another waste of my time. "No, really?"

"That sarcasm isn't going to get you far in this school."

Maybe not, but at least people will know I won't be walked on.

Coach gives me a late pass for Statistics 101 and I trudge through the nearly empty halls, regretting my next move, but someone put it in my head for a reason.

I pull out my phone and send a quick text to my dad.

> **Keeley: How much do you know about this school?**

> **I just got detention because some girl's parents basically run it.**

> **Dad: What did you do now?**

Seriously? I should have known better than to think my dad would be on my side.

> **Keeley: Nothing! But don't worry, I'll figure it out for myself. You're never there for me anyway.**

Despite a few more pings announcing incoming texts, I stuff my phone in my pocket, and get to class, so I'm not late.

A pop quiz in statistics normally wouldn't bother me, but today the bright sun captures my attention, contrasting the ominous black cloud following me around, and math is the furthest thing from my brain. I leave four of the ten problems blank. You don't need to be a mathematician to know I failed, even if I got the other six correct.

Finally, it's lunch time. Nik is nowhere in sight, so I tap my playlist. Shinedown's *Thick as Thieves* blares through the one AirPod I hide behind my hair. If teachers knew I listened to music in their classes, I'd probably be in trouble for that, too. Even though music is the only thing keeping me grounded and able to function in school. They don't care.

This is the best song for Nik and me. We had to see each other secretly the last few months in Italy and we're already planning secret outings now. I wish it didn't have to be this way, but it's plain to see that my dad will do anything to ruin my life.

The hardest part of all this? Nik and I still have an unfinished past to discuss. What if he tells me he threw my letters away? That will crush the small part of my heart that is still whole. I've almost forgotten the idea that he may have a girlfriend. He's an upstanding guy. He wouldn't be kissing me and getting way too close for my brain to function normally if he had a girlfriend. At least the Nik I once knew wouldn't.

My eyes look up from my phone, and I spot him making his way through the crowded hallway. Of course, Danny, Kyle, and Dion stick to his side. They are the only guys, besides Vinny, from the soccer team without girlfriends. They believe hanging out with my Italian Dreamboat will get them girls of their own.

Vinny, on the other hand, has declared me his conquest. He isn't quite as tall as Nik and his hair and muscles are flat, again the opposite of Nik, but I could see how a girl might find him attractive. That is until he opens his mouth.

The closer Nik gets, the faster my heart races. If I didn't know better, I'd say my anxiety was going full bore. Except this feels different. Better. My chest feels light, not a tight vise-like grip, squeezing my rib cage until all twenty-four crack under pressure.

Like magic, the crowd disappears and Nik is at my side. His arm rests high on the lockers, but his eyes stare down at me. I meet his gaze and all the misery of the morning washes away.

"Hey," he says, his voice low and dreamy. My stomach flutters and if I had to guess, so do my eyes because Nik chuckles.

"Are you ready for lunch?" he asks quickly.

I'm thankful the school has an open lunch for juniors and seniors, meaning we can leave during lunch as long as we return.

"We can eat in my truck if you want."

"S-sounds great." *Get it together, girl.*

He holds out his hand and I stare at it, like the idiot I am. *What does this mean? Only couples hold hands, right? Does he want to date? No, he's never shown interest before.* The questions are on a continuous loop in my head.

"Don't be shy. It's me. Besides, I'm trying to save you from Vinny and me from Trish. He thinks he can win you over."

A slamming locker knocks me from my trance and I scoff. "Are you afraid of a little competition?"

He takes my hand in his, lacing our fingers together like it's the most natural thing in the world, pulling me closer as he kisses my knuckles. *Keep breathing!* I take a step back to meet his eyes, but he dips toward my ear, his breath, tickling my cheek. "You're not a prize to be won," he says, his voice low and intense. "But I'll make sure if it comes to a competition, I won't lose."

Eek! Forget Jack and Rose. Our playful banter and tender moments promise a far more compelling and realistic romance, not to mention an ending where we both survive.

Before I realize how I even got to Nik's truck, he's lowering the tailgate to his shiny cobalt blue 4x4, short bed, Chevy truck. I stare at the down tailgate. "Need help?"

"No, I'm good." I set my bag down and press my hands onto the gate while I hoist my rear into place. *Shoot.* If I would have accepted his help, he would have lifted me in place. *Stupid, stupid, stupid.*

He hops up, landing flush with the side of my leg and a jolt of electricity shoots straight to my foot. *Just keep breathing.* My nerves gnaw at my stomach. There's no way I can eat, or his truck won't be so shiny anymore.

"Is it always this warm in September here?"

Nik shrugs. "I don't think it has anything to do with the weather." He wags his eyebrows at me, making me laugh. "What? Are you disagreeing?"

Definitely not. "I plead the fifth."

"We don't have that in Sicily."

"Well, you're in America now, Baby." My eyes widen, realizing my words. But in true Nik fashion, he smiles and returns to our conversation.

"This is only my second September in Maine, but warm one day and cool the next seems normal."

Really? This is only his second year at the school and everyone loves him. *Maybe something's wrong with me?*

"What's wrong?"

How does he always know? I shake my head, not wanting his pity. The peace in the air creates a familiar comfort, just like old times. The urge to ask him about his parents almost overwhelms me. Just as I build the confidence to ask, he continues with the weather.

"It's nowhere as nice as Catina." His comment reminds me of hiking Mount Etna in the fall.

"Definitely not," I agree.

I pull out my lunch and then peel off my sweatshirt; one I needed this morning to ward off the chilly air, leaving just a well-worn Shinedown T-shirt.

"Are they still your favorite band?"

"Yup." I take a bite of my apple as I swing my legs. "Do you still hate them?"

His mouth drops open. "I never hated them." I give him a pointed look that hopefully says, *Gimme a break.*

"You used those exact words." A little puff of air escapes with my laugh.

He bumps my shoulder. "Maybe it was to get a rise out of you. You're adorable when you stick up for things you believe in."

"Well, you will love the new me." When I think about what I said and his eyebrows raise, matching the playful smirk on his lips, I add, "Uh, not love me. I didn't mean that... you know, right?"

All the while I try to explain myself, he purses his lips and shakes his head playfully. It's his wink that has my heart skipping a beat. If he only knew what he's doing to me...

A sly grin rounds out his expression. *He does!*

I can't believe Nik and I are together (whatever that word means) again. Will Dad force us to leave here when he finds out? Because he will find out; he always does. So does Nik's dad. My dad is a captain in the Navy, handling many top-secret missions, so I understand his ability to find things out. Nik's dad is a different story. The man seems to know everything, yet, other than *being a boss,* Nik hasn't said anything about his dad's work.

Regardless, there aren't any excuses for either of them telling Nik and me we couldn't be together. My dad never took the time to get to know Nik in Italy. *Shocker.* He doesn't even take the time to get to know me!

Mom did, though. The five of us did everything together. Well, EJ only tagged along when dad was at work, otherwise he chose to play football or do something football related with him.

"How's your mom?" I say after swallowing my first bite. His expression sours. *Oh, no.* See, this is why I mind my own business. He tries to mask the hurt, but I see it.

He distracts himself by unwrapping his sandwich. "Mom died."

I cover my gaping mouth and rest my other hand on his forearm and he stares down at it. I slowly slide my fingers off, but his other hand traps mine between his warmth. My other hand falls to my lap. "Oh, Nik. Are you okay?"

"It was about a year ago. Mom was driving by the base and something exploded. Debris hit her car, and she lost control; drove right into a gas truck that exploded. The fire took both her and the truck driver."

"Thank God she didn't suffer."

"You don't know that!" he snaps.

I jerk back; my hand falls from his arm. He's never ever spoken to me like that. He sounds just like my dad. Nice one minute and once you let your guard down, the real beast comes out. My body instinctively tensed. *Alert, alert.* My brain is already overthinking this because that's what it does.

He hung his head. "I'm sorry. If you didn't notice, I don't count on God anymore."

"But He's still there..." my whisper mixes with nerves, wondering if he'll bite my head off again. Yes, I am a glutton for punishment.

He rests his hands on the tailgate and leans forward, swinging his legs, but not acknowledging my comment. I place my hand on his shoulder and glide it along his blades. He's my best friend. I have to overlook his outburst.

Holy muscles. It's so not fair. I shouldn't be thinking about his attractive features, begging my brain to focus instead on making him feel better.

"How's your dad handling it?"

"Like he manages everything. He worked right after we laid my mom in the ground. No concern for my feelings. He left me alone."

I know that all too well. My heart breaks for Nik.

"Is that why you came here? I assume you're with your grandparents?" I met them once when they visited their daughter and Nik in Italy. His dad seemed to tolerate them, but wasn't overly friendly. In fact, the only person I've seen him be gentle with was Rachel.

"Yeah."

We eat silently.

"It wasn't my choice to come here." He looks over his shoulder at me with dreamy chocolate eyes. They're soft, almost liquid, like melted chocolate chips.

Questions assault my brain until I let out a breath, blowing every question from my mind that would eventually cause me stomach cramps and a tight chest.

Finally, I ask, "Do you miss Italy?"

"Not right now." His hand rests on my thigh and instant heat radiates in both directions, warming my entire body. Butterflies dance in my stomach as my heart takes flight.

I begin to imagine a world where, whenever I'm having a bad day, there's someone who makes it better. A world where I can trust someone; it's such a foreign feeling. But then I realize it's always been Nik. He's never kept anything from me. That's why he's my best friend and I don't see that changing any time soon.

8

"Mᴏᴍ, I'ᴍ ʜᴏᴍᴇ!" Tʜᴇ wind steals the door from my grip and slams shut. Silence is my only response.

I check my watch. *She should have been home by now.*

My football bag lands with a thud in the kitchen as I toss the mail on the counter. An envelope addressed to me catches my eye. K. James is the name in the left corner. My heart leaps as I tear it open. *Finally.*

Keeley rose to the top of my best friend list quickly. Our connection, from football—which she called soccer—to our love for nature, hiking and music bound us together moments after meeting each other. Benito Russo, the team's sweeper, thought he could use his football position to take my girl. As if he could break through Keeley's defenses and *sweep* her right up. Nah. Our eyes met, igniting a spark that felt like a thousand exploding fireworks. Yet the silence of the past year leaves a bitter taste, making me question the meaning of our time together.

I tear open the letter and read the first line. I can't see, but my expression changes. I read the next line and my smile returned. I drop the only letter Keeley ever sent me when excessive banging jolts me.

My heart swells to know that she still considers me her best friend. She even sprayed the paper with the orchid spray I brought her for her fifteenth birthday—a few months before her dad transferred to another base.

However, her other words are troubling me. 'Why haven't you written? I think this will be my last letter. Your silence hurts too much.' Since she left, I've written Keeley twelve letters—one for each month we've been apart. Where'd they go?

Had my dad been intercepting her letters to me? Anger bubbles at the top of my chest, like hot magma brewing below Mount Etna, getting trapped in the covered-over cone. Pressure continues to build until it explodes—something I am about to do. Dad has to explain himself whenever he gets home from his month-long business trip.

Less than two seconds later, someone is banging the knocker against our wooden door even louder.

My dad drilled it into my head years ago that I should never open the door without looking at the security camera on my phone.

But the way I'm feeling right now, even organized crime bosses wouldn't mess with me.

Dad's lucky he's not here. Hopefully, for his sake, I calm down before he gets home.

"Uncle Sal, what's—" He pushes his palm into my chest, cutting off my question.

He spins, looking like a caged tiger, pacing back and forth, sweating, looking for an escape. If he doesn't stop breathing like that, he's going to hyperventilate.

I open my mouth to speak, but again he cuts me off, this time with his palm in my face. *Lord, help me have patience with him.*

"Y-y-y-your d-d-d-ad." He rubs the back of his neck.

I grip his arms, nodding my head quickly. "What about my dad?"

"H-h-he's in j-j-j-jail."

I freeze.

Jail? I narrow my eyes as he continues to explain. My arms drop to my sides. I feel my brows crease and my eyes narrow as I listen, but don't quite comprehend what Uncle Sal is saying. When he finally stops talking. I'm quiet. What could I say?

Shock isn't strong enough to describe how I feel. Sal's words play on repeat in my mind. *"This is his... third, no fourth, arrest."*

"What?"

How do I not know this already.?

I don't have to wait for my answer.

"Every time your dad went on an extended business trip..."

Uncle Sal didn't have to finish his sentence. I know. I think I always knew. The big bodyguards, cameras and money. My gut churns with my next thought. The packages. *What had I done?*

Bile rises in my throat and I push the thought away. *Lord, please forgive me for my part in this.*

"How long is his 'business trip' this time?"

He rubs his hand through his hair and shifts from one foot to the other. Tension in the air threatens to suffocate me. "Spit it out, Uncle Sal."

"Twenty to life for each count."

My stomach churns again and the bile from moments ago makes its way all the way to the trash can next to me. My mind swirls the words around. *Twenty... life... each... count...*

The knowledge I do have tells me the word count means bodies. I never imagined the man I've called, My rock... My protector... My provider... at some point in my life, could kill for a living.

"He's going to get off. His prints aren't anywhere on—"

"STOP! I don't want to hear it."

Sal slaps my upper back as I straighten to my full height, six-three. I rinse my mouth with cool, refreshing water from the kitchen sink, hoping it washes away the truths I've just learned.

"Get used to it, nephew. You're next in line to take over.

Whoa! I don't think so. "Back up. I'm sixteen. I'm not a murderer."

"Neither is your dad."

Okay. I don't understand that.

Nothing makes sense. Five minutes ago, I wanted to kill—wait, bad choice of words—fight with my dad for keeping Keeley's letters from me, and now...

Realization. Well, more of an assumption pops into my head. Dad tried to keep Keeley out of this. His sneering words, "She's too good and will keep you from taking your place in the family business one day," echo in my mind, sharp and bitter, as if spoken just yesterday.

I won't take over the family business. Not today, not tomorrow, or any day in the future.

"The plan," Uncle Sal's words pull me from my thoughts. "I'll move in here with you and prepare you for the takeover. In your dad's words, toughen you up."

I scoff. "You make it seem like I don't have a choice."

"You don't!" Sal's intense eyes are unrecognizable.

My heart stops and then races out of control. Sweat forms at my hairline. Every muscle beneath my skin trembles.

I've gone from worrying about not receiving Keeley's letters to becoming a mafia boss. *No! Never!*

"There's more." Sal's eyes lose their intensity from earlier. "Your mom..."

Right. What must she think? Did my mom put up with my dad's antics all these years, or is this something that just fell on his lap after they married? She couldn't have known before or she wouldn't have married him, right? I need to talk to her.

"She died at the hospital about an hour ago."

The sweat forming minutes earlier freezes in its place, sending a jolting chill down my spine. My body temperature plummets. I step away from Sal and cover my slacken jaw with my hand. His eyes will me to speak, but I can't. My tongue suffocates me, depriving me of the ability to speak.

Tremors run through my arms down to my hands, making them shake violently. I squeeze them under my armpits, my arms forming an X on my chest. I will the shaking to stop. Instead, I feel the vibration in my chest, a low hum that seems to shake my very bones. Emotions overwhelm me, forcing my eyes shut, blocking out the light.

Mom? Gone? How's that possible? I saw her this morning.

An unwelcome vision stabs at my heart. My mom; she's frowning. An icy dread grips in me as I watch the rain pound down on her. Her clothes, ragged and stained with something dark and unfamiliar, pierce my eyes. She starts running, the wind whipping through her hair, her arms and legs pumping furiously.

What is she running to, or away from? My heart pounds in my chest as I desperately reach for her and she vanishes around a corner. *Mom!*

Despair cripples me. Unable to move, I crumble to the floor, sobbing. I hate to cry in front of Uncle Sal. I've never seen him express empathy. He's probably thinking I'm nothing more than a child. *I don't care.* Could this day get any worse? *MOM!*

Footfalls approach me. Maybe Uncle Sal has a heart after all? He slaps me on the shoulder. "Get your crying out now. With your dad gone, you have to step up."

Shut up! My mom would never want that for me, would she? I'll never know.

A knock at the door startles me, but not as much as the pistol Uncle Sal pulls from his waistband.

"W-what are you doing?"

"Shh!" he hisses, gliding toward the door.

Another knock. "Pulizzia, open up."

Sal looks at me and returns his gun to his back, then pulls his shirt over as a cover. I imagine if the authorities catch him with a gun, he could be sitting right next to my dad.

"Ciao, ufficiali di pulizzia. Chi ti putemu fari?"

What can we do for them? Seriously? Take him too, officers. I can't stay here with him. I'll turn into a heartless, worthless excuse for a human.

I've never dealt with the authorities. Adrenaline speeds through my veins. The man's enormous hands cloud my vision. His fingers are thick sausages, ones I imagine grabbing and shaking me free from this nightmare. That would be okay.

"We need to see Nikolaus Valentino."

The authorities enter, forcing Sal to step back. When the first man reaches me, he speaks in English, but his accent is heavy. "Son, given your tears, I say you've heard the news about your parents. Do you have a relative you can contact?"

"I'm his uncle," Sal rushes over. "I'll be moving in to care for him."

The man's eyes dart toward my uncle and then focus back on me. "Do you have a nonni?"

"Yeah, my mom's parents live in America. My dad's mom lives here, but hasn't been the same since my nonno died."

"She's not capable of caring for the boy. That's why I'm moving in." Sal's nervous shifting makes my gut churn. What isn't he telling me? The pulizzia?

I study the man's face, studying Sal's.

Turning to me he says, "Please pack. You're coming with me."

Sal raises his hands. "What's going on here? His dad put me in charge of the boy while..."

The man's broad shoulders lift up and down as he laughs at Sal. "He doesn't have any say in his son's life right now."

"You'll regret this!" Sal's face turns beet-red. Mount Etna has nothing on him.

The ufficiali gets in Sal's face. My mind shoots to the gun as Sal rests his hands on his hips. "Unless you want to join your brother, don't threaten me again."

Sal clasps his hands together and begs. "Please don't take him. I have a job...I'm supposed to watch over him."

Ignoring Sal, the man turns back to me and helps me from the floor. "Go pack a suitcase. You'll be gone a long time."

9

"CAN YOU LIE DOWN back here?" I blurt out and instantly squeeze my eyes shut, realizing I sound like I'm flirting. My face is hot, but it's not the warm September sun causing my temperature to rise. In a swift motion, my palms cover my embarrassment.

With a tender touch, Nik tugs my forearms away. "You're so cute when you get flustered. Is that new or is it me?"

You. "When did you get so full of yourself?"

"When you gave me a reason to." I stare at him, unable to come up with a sarcastic remark. "But to answer your question. I don't fit back here. The specs state it's only 5'8". If you will share this tiny space with me under a sky full of stars, I'll make it work." I feel his wink in my marrow.

He gently tucks my hair behind my ear, his fingers brushing lightly against my skin. That single graze of his fingers, combined with his words, send my heart into a dizzying spiral; a rush of heat and breathlessness washes over me.

"Breathe, Keeley," Nik encourages me, caressing my back. *That's not helping.*

I take a deep breath in and exhale while he takes another bite of his Italian wafer topped with hazelnut spread and strawberries. *I miss Italian food.*

"How's your day been so far?" Nik bumps my shoulder.

Anger floods through my veins at the mere mention of my morning. He gets a text from his Uncle Sal while I'm sharing the events.

It hurts my feelings when he reads his text in the middle of my story, making doubt spread through my body faster than the rumors travel through this school. *Don't worry.* I coach myself, knowing how demanding his family is; I wouldn't want Nik to pay the consequences for not answering.

He set his phone down moments later. "No one would help with the detention?" he says without missing a beat.

"Nope. No soccer practice for me today."

Nik has his phone back in his hands; thumbs flying wildly across the screen. "We'll see about that."

"What'd you do?" I ask when he sets his phone back down and rests his hand on my thigh again.

"I texted Grayson. He's talking with his mom now."

I can't see, but I know confusion fills my expression.

"Mrs. Johnson, the vice principal, she's Grayson's mom."

A burst of excitement fills my chest. "You think that will work?"

"She's the only one who stands up to the board. For whatever reason, she's not afraid of Mr. Marsden."

"Thank you. Even if I still have detention. It means a lot that you'd try to help me."

He places what's left of his sandwich down and turns his body to face me. "I'd do anything for you, Keeley."

His words puncture my heart. His eyes dip to my lips and my heart races out of control. I've only kissed one person. I still haven't forgotten the dreadful experience. If the time ever comes, what if Nik thinks I'm a horrible kisser?

My eyes drift toward our touching legs, not ready to find out. "I'm sorry I didn't show that last day in Italy, but it wasn't because I didn't want to. I couldn't."

Nik lifts my chin with his finger. "Why?"

"My dad took my Vespa. I accused him of doing it to keep me from you. Of course, he denied it." I huff out a breath. "I drove out there later that evening."

"You did?"

I nod. He doesn't seem to believe me, so I reach underneath the collar of my t-shirt and pull out the locket. The light touch of his fingers inadvertently touching my collarbone as he opens the locket sends shivers down my spine.

"I haven't taken it off since that day."

He rests his forehead on mine as he closes the pendant, and it falls back in place. "I waited as long as I could in the pouring rain. My dad made me—" He stops himself. "I'm so sorry, I couldn't wait longer. I had so much to tell you."

"We're here now." The words hang heavy in the air between us. *Wait!* Maybe I don't want him to tell me. It's probably bad since he didn't write.

"Keeley, stop overthinking this."

"I'm not—" My protest is weak. What can I say? I'm not good at lying.

"What if I told you I had planned on telling you I *like* you?"

His confession hangs in the air, and my tongue catches in my throat. Is he serious? *Yes, he is! Duh. Didn't you hear the way he said "like?"* Apparently, I'm the last to grasp this.

But how does he feel now?

He leans closer. *Don't overthink it.* Nik's kiss will make today perfect. Our breath mingles. His is warm and welcoming.

How will we be together? My dad wouldn't let us be friends in Italy. He'll never let me be his girlfriend.

Briiing! The lunch bell startles me and we bump noses. "Oh, I'm so sorry." I hide my face with my hands again.

"Nothing to be sorry for." He pulls my hands away from my face and hops to the ground, tugging me from the tailgate.

He pulls me in for a hug, wrapping his arms around my shoulders. I let my arms curl around his waist and my cheek finds the perfect spot—right in the center.

"I'm so glad we are together again. We'll figure out a way to be together." He kisses the top of my head and releases me.

After shutting the tailgate, he holds out his hand and I take a deep breath. I don't hesitate to lace our fingers together. He's all I've ever wanted. I exhale a shaky breath. Can this really be happening? Will Nik and I finally get our chance to be more than friends?

10

"Whatever you said or did, thank you," Keeley smiles at Grayson. "I guess your mom really doesn't like Trish."

I thought Keeley looked good at fourteen. Add three more years, more curves, a few more freckles, and she's absolutely stunning. Her practice jersey doesn't do her justice, but her shorts reveal her toned legs. I hate thinking about the comments I've heard in the locker room. To be fair, the guys have made the same observations about Keeley that I have, but again, she's mine and tonight, everyone, including her, will know it.

"No problem. My mom hates injustices and Trish seems to be involved in a lot of them."

Nik slaps him on the shoulder. "Yeah, thanks."

Grayson shrugs it off and sprints away.

"You know getting you out of detention was completely selfish on my part, right?"

She has said nothing about me liking her. Suppose her feelings are different? Or worse, what if she doesn't wish to be friends again?

"I hope you don't regret it. You could get sick of me."

I throw her a playful smile. "Never."

Her breath hitches. The way her body responds to me does a lot for my ego. Other girls respond similarly, but it doesn't hit my heart in the same way. Keeley is my girl. She is, in my head at least, and it will soon be official. That way, I can protect her.

The coach blows his whistle and I pull Keeley in for a quick hug before we run onto the field. We're both very competitive, so we learned a long time ago that in order to preserve our friendship, what happens on the field has to stay there.

"Get a room." Vinny's disgusted tone irks me. I clench my jaw so hard I think I crack a tooth. But a quick glance at Keeley running by my side and I'm able to overlook even his nasty comment.

We huddle around Coach Bucci. He's sharing highlights from our last game.

My mind drifts to Keeley's hug; I can still feel the warmth of her embrace. In that short time, my mind captured every nuance. The way her soft body blended with my muscles sent a wave of relaxation through me. I breathed her in, and the delicate, floral scent of orchids, like a whisper, clung to her hair. Her palms grazed my back, a gentle caress that felt like the softest silk.

"Now with Keeley, we shouldn't have that problem," Coach finishes, clapping his hands together to punctuate his statement.

Problem? *What problem?* Everyone lines up for drills. I'll have to figure that out later.

We're nearing the end of practice, but adrenaline affords me hours of playtime. Keeley's amazing athleticism and fierce determination ignite a desire within me, spreading like wildfire; all other thoughts snuffed out.

Until, Vinny's condescending taunt, "She'll never choose you over me," surge through my veins, so potent I want to throttle him.

"Keeley, show us your scissor kick," Coach orders.

She glances my way and I send her an encouraging smile like I did when I helped her perfect this skill. That memory pulls me away to my backyard in Sicily.

"Please don't kick me," I say, one hand covering my face and my other covering my family jewels as my dad refers to them. "Okay, go." My words muffle behind my hand, making Keeley laugh.

I spread my fingers wide to watch. She jumps in the air looking like she's about to do a jumping roundhouse kick and swings her non-kicking leg upward, giving her the momentum with her body to swing and rotate in mid-air just like I taught her. She kicks the ball with her laces, careening it into the goal.

"Yes," she yells and fist bumps the air.

I cheer and run to her, lifting her in a hug, swinging her around. "That was great. Next time, keep your non-kicking leg a little ahead of your kicking leg to give you more power."

In that instant, I realized Keeley was perfect for me. After that day, she got awkward and shy whenever we were together.

"Valentino, are you with us?!"

I rub my hands over my face, bringing me back to the present, and nod. So much has happened in the last three years. I have so many questions for her, but whenever we're together, she steals my breath away—*Ugh!*

Keeley performs flawlessly, giving the haters more ammunition, but I storm after her, lift her off the ground and swing her around. "You were magnificent." She blushes when I wink at her.

Coach splits the team into first and second string, setting us up for a 7v7 scrimmage. "Allen, Cameron, get to the goals." Allen is the first string goalie, Cameron second. The first couple of games, Cameron kept the other team from scoring, but the coach didn't put him in quick enough and we lost by one goal. If Allen doesn't focus, he could ride the bench more.

"Get your head in the game, Valentino."

I shake my head. "Yes, coach!" I better listen to my own advice before I'm benched, too.

Keeley gives me a concerned look, her eyes asking if I am okay. I smile and give her a quick thumbs up as I take my position on the field. In true Keeley fashion, she claps her hands together and yells, "Let's go."

For whatever reason, Coach Bucci has Vinny with the second string players and he is on me instantly, taunting me about Keeley. "What were you doing, Valentino? Thinking about how I'm going to steal Keeley?" He shoves his shoulder into my chest, kicking the ball up the field.

I might thrash that kid!

I sprint after the ball, but Keeley beats me there and takes possession. Vinny is all over her. I'm not an idiot. He's enjoying the physical contact he's creating, and it takes every inch of my willpower not to take him down.

Keeley kicks the ball down the field to Kyle, playing center back. He kicks and Cameron blocks the shot.

I know Cameron is going to kick it high and short, so I rush to regain possession. Vinny and I have the same thought, but I'm stronger and faster, so I have the ball. Then the dirtbag says, "Don't leave your girlfriend alone at the party next week, or you'll find her with me."

I don't have time to think. I kick the ball haphazardly. It could be in the bushes for all I know, and Vinny's off the ground, both my fists clenching his shirt. "You better stay away from her or I'll mess you up!"

Vinny's flailing arms are trying to reach for my jersey, but he's definitely not succeeding.

It's only the sound of Coach Bucci's whistle less than a foot from me that brings me from my angered state.

"Valentino! Get ahold of yourself" He pulls on my arm, but Coach isn't able to budge me either.

"Do you know what this dirtbag said?" I roar.

"Let him go, Nikolaus," Kyle flanks me on the other side.

I repeat what Vinny said, and the dirtbag laughs. "What, you can't handle the truth?" He's testing me.

"Vinny, shut up," Coach Bucci instructs.

Finally, someone with some sense.

"Nikolaus, you hit Keeley," Kyle says, still trying to get Vinny free, but my hands are vise grips.

My head whips in her direction. Her palms are covering her face. Aurora and Beryl surround her with towels.

"You're lucky I can't finish you off now." With an exaggerated shove further in the air, I drop Vinny to the ground and rush to Keeley's side.

"I am so sorry. I lost control of the ball."

Keeley looks up at me, a bloody towel under her nose, trying to capture the rushing fluid. "It looks like you lost control of more than the ball."

Mannaggia! She's right. Would knowing the whole story matter to her?

"If you knew what Vinny said—"

"It doesn't matter." *She wouldn't say that if she knew.* Unless she's changed, Keeley was saving herself for marriage.

Coach blows his whistle. "Bring it in."

I cup her elbow and press my hand to her lower back, guiding her toward center field. Thankfully, she hasn't pushed me away.

Coach Bucci waits until everyone gathers around him. "Practice is over for today. Everyone better play as a team this coming week. We have our regular games and one make-up game from two weeks ago. We shouldn't have any trouble beating this team if you work together."

Vinny smirks at me as he leaves the field. When I turn back to Keeley, planning to help her to the locker room, she's gone. I know she's probably wondering what made me lose control. If I tell her, it will embarrass her. If I don't, she'll be mad at me.

I race ahead, catching up with her. "Let me help you to the locker room," I offer, cupping her elbow to steady her as she walks.

"Thank you. I forgive you. What happens on the field..."

She smiles up at me, and I melt.

When we reach the locker room door, EJ comes rushing over and I explain what happened. For siblings, they have very different reactions. Keeley's eyes are as big as plates and her cheeks are red with what I know is embarrassment. EJ's eyes are dark like a soldier ready to attack and his face is red with what I know is anger, because I imagine that was the color of my face a few moments ago.

"Isn't this a Christian school?"

EJ and I share a look. My heart thumps for my sweet, naïve Keeley. Not only do guys think differently than girls, but just because someone attends a Christian school, that doesn't mean they are an active follower. *Look at me.* The thought jolts me. What if Keeley doesn't want to be around me now that I've stopped calling on the Lord?

"Maybe Vinny needs the football team to teach him a lesson."

I appreciate EJ is her brother, but I want to protect her, and I tell him as much.

"We can join forces, but whenever anyone disrespects my sister, I take that as a personal hit against me and I will make that person pay."

The look on EJ's face tells me he's not just talking about Vinny.

"I hear you loud and clear, EJ." Hurting Keeley is not an option. No problem there.

He nods and says, "Good," before entering the locker room.

My eyes stare down at Keeley. "I promise you I'd never hurt you."

She raises her hand to my cheek and instinctively, I lean in, embracing the warmth of her hand and a little blood, but that doesn't matter. "You already have. Now go change, you stink." She laughs.

"That's not something you can just say and expect me to leave."

"But you really stink." She winks at me, sending my heart into arrhythmia. Clearly, my brain hasn't informed my vital organs with the seriousness of her words.

"I don't want you alone with Vinny around. You'll wait for me, right?"

Talk about Déjà vu. I'm asking her to wait for me when I chose not to wait for her years ago. Does she still hold that against me? Is that what she meant by, *"You already have?"*

My jaw clenches, waiting for her to answer.

"Yes."

Perfect. I won't make her wait anymore. She's had some time to get settled into her new place. Now I'm going to make her mine.

11

I NEVER THOUGHT GETTING up for school could be so easy. Etna hasn't arrived when I park my truck and the cool October air whips across my face as I exit. My feet carry me across the parking lot all the way to Keeley's locker.

The piece of paper I prepared for her shakes in my hand. *What if she says no?*

The emptiness of this hall resonates with my heart in a way I don't like. Ever since meeting Keeley in Italy, I've known what it means to care for someone. Sadly, I've also known what an empty heart feels like.

Here's goes nothing. I push the paper into her locker and listen for the light thump as it hits the bottom.

Now, I need a good place to watch. Keeley is absolutely adorable, especially when she doesn't think people are watching.

Five minutes later, Keeley and EJ are at their lockers. My note falls to the ceramic tile floor and Keeley looks at it and then to the left and the right before bending over to pick it up.

I chuckle. *What does she think it is?*

Her shoulder slumps against her locker as she reads. The pink rising in her cheeks is a good sign.

Is she rereading it? It takes so long for her eyes to lift from my written words. If we are going to move forward, it's time to get my answer.

I sneak out from the stairwell when she turns into her locker, putting what she needs for class in her backpack. EJ spots me and I motion for him to stay quiet.

My hands cover Keeley's eyes, causing her to jump a little.

"Who's there?"

EJ calls over from his locker. "You need to guess, Kee."

"Um, okay. Is it Billy? No wait, this is Zayn. No, not the right scent." I sniff myself. This morning I put on the ocean scent she loves. *What the heck?*

"Come on, Kee. It shouldn't be that hard." EJ is moving closer; the smirk on his face says he's enjoying this a little too much. What I don't know is if he's enjoying his sister's pain or if they're working together against me.

She sighs and leans back into my chest, igniting the skin underneath my sweatshirt. "Ooh, this has to be David."

My patience has its limits and I've gone beyond that. "Are you serious, Keeley?" My hands drop and she turns toward me.

"Oh, Nik. Has it been you the whole time?" She's fighting a smile.

But when EJ fist bumps her, I realize they were playing me from the beginning.

"You should have seen the expression on your face. Compared to you, even a lost puppy with its big, sad eyes welling with tears wouldn't look as broken-hearted as you."

Whatever. "Thanks, EJ. What about the bro code?"

"Sorry, blood's thicker water."

I force a smile, hoping he can't see the hurricane winds storming inside me. My blood, as EJ says, wants me to kill people for a living. I can only imagine what it would be like to have a family like Keeley and EJ.

They high five one more time before EJ returns to his locker.

I'll take all the razzing Keeley dishes out if she laughs like this all the time. But you know what they say about payback...

I invade her space. The pulse in her neck, clearly visible when her zip up sweatshirt slips off her shoulder slightly and the v-neck athletic shirt she's wearing exposes most of her collarbone.

Keeley needs to be nurtured and shown how special she is. Of course, I want her to be my girlfriend. I've wanted that since the day I left the locket she's wearing on our tree near Mount Etna. But if I blurt that out too soon, I could scare her away. Our friendship is as strong as ever, so I won't risk that.

"Do you have an answer for me?" My finger gestures towards the letter she clenches desperately.

As she leans against the locker, the softness in her eyes fans the embers of hope back to life within me.

Please say yes. It's a rare Thursday we don't have practice. Coach has an appointment that he says he can't miss.

"I'd love to hang out tonight, but I'm painting my nails."

Hmmm. "Is that the same thing as saying you're washing your hair so you can avoid a date?" I feel victorious when she bites back a smile.

"Is this a date?"

"Do you want it to be?"

She giggles and holds up the note. "You asked me, so it's only fair you answer."

I grab the note, place it inside her book, and quickly cup her face with that same hand, letting it linger when her breath hitches. "I've wanted a date with you for as long as I can remember."

I grab her bag and sling it over my shoulder, shut her locker door, and hold out my hand for her.

"Perfect. It sounds like we'll have a great night." Her breathy response carries me through the rest of the day.

12

SITTING ON THE COUCH in flannel lounge pants and the shirt and sweatshirt I wore to school, I open my nail caddy, displaying all my nail polish. I select a light blue. Not only will it match my jersey, it's bright and makes me feel happy.

Words cannot convey the essence of my joy... Well one word can, Nik!

He dropped me off earlier, leaving EJ Etna to drive home when football practice gets out. I didn't object to riding home with Nik and EJ never protests driving.

My parents left this morning for an overnight stay in the mountains to celebrate their anniversary. They left me in charge of dinner. I texted EJ and asked him to pick up pizza on the way home. He didn't object to that either.

The ringing doorbell makes me flinch. A streak of nail polish marks my skin. I sigh and cap the nail polish before I trudge to the door.

Through a gap in the curtain, I see the upper half of a familiar body. *He's back.* I look down at my clothes. Good grief.

"Is everything okay, Nik?" I holler through the door.

"Yeah. I'm here for our date."

Date? "We have a date tonight?" He must have lost it. I would have remembered a date with Nikolaus Valentino.

"Gee, thanks. "I guess I'm just...forgettable," he mumbles and my heart stings.

Oh, don't sell yourself short, handsome. I've never forgotten you. I peel back the curtain. "Nik, you didn't say the date was for tonight."

A sheepish smile slowly filled his face. "What can I say? I wanted to surprise you. Can I please come in? I brought your favorite."

My eyes lock in on the half gallon tub. Oreo, cookie dough ice cream. *Mmmm.*

"I'm not sure this is a good idea," I say opening the door, "but if you have nothing better to do than watch me eat ice cream and paint my nails, so be it."

Twenty minutes later, we've eaten the ice cream. "I forgot how much you like ice cream," Keeley said to Nik, taking the empty container, letting our fingers brush against each other. Our eyes catch and his are filled with the tenderness I remember.

When I return, I douse a cotton pad with nail polish remover while I dig deep, finding the courage to find out if he considers this a date.

"Thank you for the ice cream. I would have liked to dress a little better for our first date and cover this." I gesture toward my black eye, An unintentional gift from Nik.

"That mark only adds to your character and beauty."

Ahh. "Thank you."

"First date?" He nudges my shoulder. "Are you saying they'll be more?" His voice has dropped even more since we last saw each other in Italy, causing my insides to feel like magma.

I bow my head. "Not necessarily. Especially if ice cream isn't involved."

"I'll always have ice cream for you. That's what friends are for, right?"

A flicker of fog rolls a memory away. "Nik, did you ever consider me a friend?"

"My best friend. No cap."

Nik's never lied to me, so I believe him now. It doesn't make sense that he didn't write if he considered me his best friend. Unfortunately, I don't have a chance to ask him anything else because EJ comes home with pizza.

"Hey. I didn't expect you, Nik."

My heart races. "He stopped by. Apparently, I messed up and we had... have... are on... a date. But I'd already planned to paint my nails..."

I'm still rambling about who knows what. EJ looks bored; Nik amused.

While I'm talking, Nikolaus grabs the now dried white pad from me and pours on the liquid. His warm hand tenderly takes mine.

My breath hitches, causing me to pause for a moment.

"I'll eat in my room," EJ says as he leaves.

Once EJ's gone, Nik says, "Tell me how things are going with your dad."

"P-uh." I shake my head. "When I was little, I wanted his attention so badly. I did everything to be a good girl just so he'd spend time with me, but he didn't. He always had something to do. So, one time

I used markers to color all over the walls, the couch, and myself. That got his attention, but I got yelled at and that made me a little scared and jumpy. Then I decided to try joking with him."

"Your dad doesn't seem like the joking type," Nik sets the pad down and puts lotion in his hand and starts massaging my hands. I give him a questioning look. "I watched my mom get one too many manicures apparently."

"I'm not complaining. This is calming." I take a deep breath. "Anyway, he's not. My dad can tease, as he calls it, but if I tease him back, he gets mad saying that I don't know how." I shrug, the heaviness of the painful memories weigh me down again. "So now, I keep to myself, not wanting to be let down again. Once we left Italy, he started pressing me with questions about my life, but I don't have a desire to spend time with him and be put down, told my opinions are stupid, or be yelled at. It's like that old song *Cats in the Cradle.* I shrug again, blinking to fight the tears.

Despite the tough topic, my breathing and heart aren't speeding out of control like they usually do when my thoughts get away from me. Every muscle is relaxed. Nik's warm fingers feel like the black sand around Mount Etna that burned my hands the first time he and his mom brought me. How was I supposed to know that Etna had erupted a few months before we arrived and the rocks slightly below the surface were still warm. I remember how he dumped his ice water in a bag and stuffed my hand inside it. My hand sure isn't ice now. Neither is my face. Based on the heat I feel, it's probably one shade away from crimson.

Nik must feel the tension too since he clears his throat.

I begin throwing questions at Nik. Questions about his grandparents and dad, our history project, and all the girls competing for his attention.

He stops my incessant questioning by placing his finger to my lips. The way he's looking at me isn't demeaning like he's trying to silence me. It's tender and full of affection, so much that I can almost feel myself melting. Kissing me is the only other way I can think of that will keep me quiet. But I don't suggest this or move closer to make my daydream become a reality. If he wants to kiss me he will and if he doesn't, I can continue to torture myself dreaming about it. Way. Too. Much.

I mean who has these strong feelings for their best friend? Apparently me. When we had lunch in his truck he'd said he was going to tell me that he <u>liked</u> me. But he hasn't brought it up again. Did he change his mind?

Each slow, deliberate touch is a spark; a waging war between reason and instinct. I desperately want to believe Nik is affected by this, too.

Nik picks up the blue nail polish bottle and unscrews the cap. Shock isn't a strong enough word to describe how I feel that he's painting my nails, or that it's coming out much better than I imagined.

"If we're friends, why didn't you write?"

His eyes meet mine with a swirl of confusion. As he picks up my next hand, my phone buzzes. I peek at it. Mom. "I have to get that."

"Hey."

"Keeley, you need to get Nik out of the house right now."

How does she know he's here? *EJ. The rat.*

"Your dad is taking a shower and his phone buzzed with activity. You're just lucky I looked before he did. I don't know if he has it on record and can check it or what, so..."

I hope Mom isn't mad at me. I hadn't planned any of this. Equally as nerve racking, my dad never told me he had cameras monitoring us around the clock.

"He's as good as gone. I love you."

"I love you too, Sweetheart."

I set my phone on the coffee table and bolt from my seat. "I'm sorry, but you have to go." I explain what my mom said and walk him to the door.

"May I at least hug you?"

At least?

I nod.

He steps in and his strong arms wrap around my shoulders, mine scrap his sides and rest on his lower back, while his chest supports my head. My heart is beating as wildly as his. For a guy with strong arms, this hug feels tender, almost intimate, the way a boyfriend would hug his girlfriend when leaving her house.

But that's not what this is.

Could it be? This hug is lasting longer than I've ever hugged any other guy before. "I'll go because I don't want you to get in trouble, but we have to talk and I want to spend more time with you."

I reluctantly let go when Nik releases me. "We have our project to work on, so we'll see each other for that."

Really? He says something sweet and I mention some stupid school assignment.

"I've never been so happy to work."

Eek!! Words no longer exist for me.

Nik kisses me on the cheek. "You and me, the party tomorrow, right?"

"I wouldn't miss it."

In less than five minutes, I can no longer see any remnant of Nik in the driveway or the house, but I can smell him. I close my eyes and imagine myself in his arms again. My favorite place in the world.

13

"You must think you're a big deal, stealing Nik," Trish flanks Keeley's side opposite me.

"Get lost, Trish." I know Keeley can handle the mean girl herself, but I want to show her I can be her best friend and her boyfriend. I've been walking her to every class and meeting her when the class is over. I want to show her how I feel since every time I try to talk about it, her breathing escalates and she gets that deer in the headlights look.

Tonight, I've been extra vigilant, making sure Vinny keeps his distance.

"Slumming doesn't look good on you, Nik."

I squeeze Keeley's hand, hoping she doesn't take Trish's words seriously.

"Well, Trish," Keeley says, voice laced with amusement, "neither does that shirt, but you still wore it."

"Oh, burrrn." Kyle and Dion fist bump to the side of us.

"I've never known you to be mean." I lean and whisper in her hair.

Her green eyes lock on mine. "No one's ever dissed you before."

Trish was dissing her. But I don't mention that. I find her naiveté adorable, except when she's questioning my feelings for her. Kee sticking up for me warms my insides.

I pull her hand to my chest and place it over my heart. It's beating rapidly for her and I want her to know it.

It's been nearly two weeks of Trish shooting icy daggers at Keeley when we walk down the hallway. The dance captain's animosity hangs heavy in the air as she glares at Keeley with narrow eyes and a sour expression like she ate an entire package of Sour Patch Kids.

"You think you're something special, don't you? Getting Principal Johnson to change my classes. What's the matter, couldn't take a little competition?"

Keeley laces our fingers together and smirks at Trish. "I've already won the big score." With a soft smile, she lifts our joined hands to her mouth, pressing a tender kiss to my knuckles. "I didn't think you'd be up for losing anything else?"

"Well, I never..." Trish storms off.

"It's been too long then," Kyle yells from behind, surprising us. He shrugs. "She's been mean to me since middle school when the rumor got around that I liked her... A little bit of justice is finally served."

I lean over and whisper in Keeley's hair, breathing in the faint orchid smell I've grown to love and associate with her and our time together in Italy. "Don't let her bother you. She's a simp."

Keeley gently scolds me, tossing her head toward me. "Be nice." Her Mediterranean green eyes beg me to be nice. *Nice, huh?* The thought of kissing her until the world disappears would qualify, right?

I shrug. "No one picks on my girl. Are you doing okay?"

Her rapid breathing catches my attention. Keeley's darting eyes concern me. Last week, she told me that right before an anxiety attack, sometimes she feels like everyone is staring at her and the walls around her close in, depriving her lungs of essential air. Her palm is sweaty and her breathing sounds shallow.

"Keeley, are you okay?"

She shakes her head gently. "Burning... Lungs... Need... Air."

I tighten my hand around Keeley's as I move her through the groups of teenagers dancing, and past a table with bottled water. I swipe one and lead her to the backdoor.

Outside I find a spot for ourselves. "Breathe." I start breathing the way she should, in through the nose and slowly out the mouth. All the while my hand gently rubs her back.

A few minutes later, her breathing slows and is finally controlled. I open a bottle of water and hand it to her. I know she could have done that herself, but I want to take care of her.

"Thanks." She takes a small sip. "I'm sorry. I let her get in my head with her perfectly painted nails and... I don't know."

I can't let that slide. "*Perfectly painted nails?* I think yours are lit compared to hers."

She laughs. *Yes, exactly what I wanted.* "I did have the best nail stylist in all of Maine paint mine, so I think you're right."

"Just Maine? Not the world?"

Keeley shakes her head. "My apologies. The best stylist in the universe."

"That's better." I wink at her and enjoy watching the blush rise in her cheeks. "Wanna dance?" My head jerks toward the center of the patio.

"Here?"

"No, on the moon."

She playfully shoves my arm. I let her move it back a little, but I grip her wrist with gentle hands and pull her toward my chest. "Of course here."

Holding her in my arms sends liquid courage through my veins. "Keeley how come we haven't talked about our last day in Italy?"

Her head is nestled on my shoulder. I swear she sniffed me, but I can't be sure.

As we sway to the music, I grip her tighter, drawing my strength from the strongest person I know.

"I'm scared," she whispers.

I pull her away from me, so I can see her eyes. "Scared of what?"

She pulls her lip in with her teeth, distracting me in the best possible way. *Get your head in the game, Valentino!* I repeat the advice Coach gave me not long ago.

"I thought I lost you forever," she says, wrapping her fingers tighter around my biceps.

"For a very smart girl, you've kinda missed everything."

Throwing her hands on her hips she murmurs, "Well, why don't you fill me in?"

"Fine," I mock her tone. "I told you I liked you and you haven't said anything about it. If anyone should be scared, it should be me. You've left me wondering if I've lost my best friend."

Her eyes widen, and disbelief washes over her, twisting her mouth into an awestruck O. "I've been nervous that you changed your mind or... Hey what did you tell EJ. He said you wouldn't let him say anything."

"I should have known—"

Keeley shook her head. "He only told me that he couldn't tell me anything, so he was more loyal to you than me."

An amused grin makes her even more beautiful. "Nikolaus Valentino, are you blushing?"

"What?! No." I dip my chin, but Keeley is ruthless. She steps forward, our feet touching and she places her palm on my jaw. She captivates me with the powerful scent of orchids. I haven't moved my head; her lips are within reach. My heart throbs with happiness.

"I thought we were best friends again?"

I pin her with my eyes. "Again? It never stopped for me."

Her smile gives me the encouragement I need. "I told EJ that I was going to do whatever it took to make you my girl."

"As in girlfriend?" Her voice, a combination of surprise and questioning makes the corners of my mouth quirk up.

I shake my head, "Yes, Keeley," I say and let a breathy chuckle escape after I answer.

"Sorry, just making sure."

The muscle in my jaw is twitching. "So, what do I need to do or say to convince you?"

As if I pulled her from a trance, she smiles. "Nothing. I've always wanted to be yours."

Happiness trembles inside of me. Everyone around us fades away as I brush my knuckles down her cheek and then leaning in, I whisper, "*Trattu comu la principìssa ca si, Keeley mia.*"

Her hand drops to my forearm, instantly transferring the heat from my cheek to its new location.

"I'm afraid, my Sicilian is a little rusty, could you translate please?" Her breath tickles the skin on the side of my neck just as a spark from the firepit pops and escapes its stone home.

"I will treat you like the princess you are, my Keeley."

Her shoulders relax. "Aw."

She rises to her tiptoes. *I've waited three years to kiss this—my girl.*

"It looks like you finally told her," EJ's booming voice not a foot away steals the moment.

"Yup." I hang my head.

"I'm heading to the bathroom," her voice soft and eyes pinned on me. "And you better be gone when I get back," she says to EJ with authority.

"Just upholding my brotherly responsibility. You'll need someone to help you sneak around without Dad catching on."

Her face pales, the blood seeming to flee from her cheeks, leaving behind a ghostly white *Why did EJ have to bring up their dad?* Her mouth sets in a hard line.

"It'll be okay, Keeley," I say, stepping forward with my arms spread wide. She steps into them willingly.

I kiss the top of her head. "Everything will work out. Don't worry." *I know that's like telling a clock not to tell the time.*

She's finally mine, and I'll take care of her from this day forward.

First, I have to get my stuff in order and I know just where to start.

14

THE DIM LIGHTS INSIDE Dion's house make the room seem eerily creepy. *Hi anxiety, what brings you to play again today?* Maybe if I treat it with the same sarcasm as I do my dad, it will disappear and all but ignore me just like he does.

Or not. My sweaty palms and heart thumping against my ribs has me searching for the nearest exit. Nik will look for me in his truck...eventually.

If only my dad had been as persistent. He nags me now that I'm older, but he didn't want anything to do with me when I was younger. At this point, he just wants to show his authority. If he finds out about Nik and me... *No daughter of mine will date before she can file for Social Security.* He thinks he's funny, but he's not. Especially since he let me date one of his buddies' kids. That didn't turn out so well, since the guy hurt me and made me feel just as insecure as my dad does. *Thank goodness for you, Lord, helping me to see I'm imperfectly perfect, just the way you created me.*

The thought of my dad ramps up my anxiety. Most often I listen to it. Actually, that sounds too pleasant and polite. In reality, I bow down to it and worship it—the opposite of what I am supposed to do. First Peter tells us to cast our anxieties on to God and He will take care of us. Just this week I heard a podcast that said if we give our worries to God, but we still fret over them then we don't actually trust God with our problems. So guess what I've been doing since I heard that? Yup, that's right—worrying about how God will forgive me because I keep letting my anxiety get the best of me.

I freeze before I can reach the bathroom. Not only would I have to pass Trish Marsden who's hanging all over the captain of the football team (I don't care. At least it's not my brother, or Nik), but worse than her (yes, there is someone worse)...Vinny.

Don't freak out. Walk. Good advice for someone who listens to rational comments. That's not me. Instead, my teeth grind into my lip and my hands grip the hem of my shirt until my knuckles hurt. *Maybe there's another bathroom?* I ponder things too long and Vinny strolls toward me with an open beer in his hand.

Nothing gets me out of an anxiety funk (I don't like the word attack) faster than an injustice. Before he can say a word, I pounce.

"You're drinking? Athletes aren't allowed to drink. Everyone knows it ruins performance." He takes a gulp. *Gross!* "That means you must've taken up drinking a long time ago, huh?" I look around. He's the only one with alcohol. Something seems off.

He smirks and tips the can back, guzzling the remainder of its contents. He winces, almost like he doesn't like the taste, before slamming the now empty can on the side table. Vinny stares at me with dark, stormy eyes, like a fox after its prey, making me wonder if the consequences for my sarcasm will be worth the two point three seconds of happiness it brought me in the moment. He wipes his chin of beer residue as he takes short, calculated steps toward me without breaking eye contact.

Sweat trickles down my back as a bomb of dread explodes in my belly. *Lord, you're there? Please send help.* Guilt swirls around my heart realizing God was telling me to leave earlier. I should have listened to my body.

Sometime during my plea for help and criticizing myself, Vinny snuck up on me. Now his beer stained breath is way too close, sending waves of nausea through my abdomen. If I'm lucky, I'll have second hand drunkenness and throw up on him. Is that even a thing?

Now it is. The little bit I ate for dinner before meeting Nik is on Vinny's shoes.

"What the—"

"My body can't take the smell of booze." I offer as an apology. Vinny's shadow looms closer. He's been a thorn in my side since I arrived. The end of his torment, is feeling more like the beginning of something worse.

He slips out of his sneakers and makes his way around my mess and is back in my space again. Normally, I'd be embarrassed with my vomit breath, but maybe it will act as a repellent for the jerk standing in front of me.

"You don't know it yet, but you're going to be mine."

Ew! Those words were so romantic coming from Nik, but from Vinny, they sound gross, disgusting, and somehow, borderline illegal.

"Come on. Let's go make out." He attempts to brush his fingers on my cheek, but I smack his arm away with a force strong enough for anyone to see it is rejection.

"Are you drunk?" That's a stupid question. Of course he is.

"Not too drunk to know what I want... and that's you." His speech slurs enough to discredit his words.

My eyes scan the room, but all I see are floaters and fuzzy walls closing in around me. Is anyone going to help or are they too busy swallowing each other's tonsils? *I knew I should have stayed home.*

Again my troubled thoughts put me in danger. Vinny hoists me over his shoulder. "You're coming with me."

Please, Lord. Get me out of this situation.

I screech half surprised, but mostly scared. I've never been in a situation like this, but I've been warned. Dad will never know that this happened because somehow it will be my fault for not listening to him and staying in my room until I found a good guy to marry or died, even though he's been pushing for me to socialize. He's for real despite being illogical. Obviously, I can't find a guy if I don't leave my room. But this is why I don't go out.

Pounding on Vinny's back and kicking my legs do little to deter his determination. I can't see where he's taking me, but something more bothersome is that no one is helping me. Are these people so immune to anyone else's life that they ignore someone in trouble even when they are in the same room? What has this world come to?

Lord, I know you hear me. I reach around and claw at his face. Vinny swears and nearly drops me.

"HEY!" Vinny freezes when someone hollers his name. "My mind recognizes that voice. *Thank you, Lord, for answering my prayers.*

It wasn't the voice I'd expected or hoped for, but my second choice for sure.

"Put my sister down!"

Until he puts me down, I can't see anything. I should be relieved when my feet touch the floor, but the entire football team, or at least the players at the party, created a circle around Vinny and me, which brought all the other teens' attention to me as well. My heart was already pounding like a drum in my chest, but now it's racing like thunder in a storm, like it's trying to flee my body.

"Everything's fine, fellas. It's not what it looks like. Isn't that right, sweetness."

Ew, again. I shove away from Vinny and he stumbles backward, allowing me to bolt. Gasping, I flee to my brother, his arm a lifeline sent from heaven.

"Is Nik still outside?" he asks quietly while the guys intimidate Vinny some more.

I shrug, afraid if I speak, the tears stinging at the corner of my eyes will spill down to my cheeks and I will never give anyone here that satisfaction.

"EJ, come back here," Dion yells. "It's Nik."

"Come on, Keeley; stay with me. Guys, don't let him move." EJ throws orders around to me then his teammates like he's a king.

What I see in the backyard is unexpected. I drop EJ's hand and he takes off running, while useless ole me stares, frozen in the last spot my feet touched, rapid-fire breathing assaulting my exhausted lungs. I belong back in my room listening to music, but instead here I am watching Nik pulverize someone. Why? I wish I knew.

Emotions sit on my chest like the twenty pound blanket I drape over me at night so I can sleep. I've played pretend long enough tonight. That's right. I pretended that I could function like most teenagers. I pretended that I enjoyed being at this party, and I pretended that the flirty moments between Nik and I could move beyond friendship. I was wrong on all accounts and now I'm ready to return to reality.

"What are you doing, man?" EJ tugs on Nik's arm to stop him, but Nik shoves him away.

"Watch it. I don't know what's going on here and frankly, I don't care—"

"You will." Nik's heaving chest and the dripping anger in his tone is something I've seen too much lately and would be perfectly fine never seeing it again.

Nik grabs the guy's hair and pulls his head back, forcing him to look my brother in the face. "Tell him why you deserved every punch and then beg him not to hit you, too."

When the guy, whose face is dripping with blood, doesn't say anything, Nik tugs a little harder, pulling him to his feet and the boy grunts in pain.

"It was only a joke."

Pain thrashed through my entire body. An invisible vise grip squeezes the life out of my core while my limbs render numb. No matter what this guy has to say, I don't think it warrants rearranging his face.

Nik's eyes—raging with hatred—are seared into my memory, petrifying me. I swear he's a different person. Has his mother's death changed him that much? A better question: do I want to be friends with anyone who can act like this? He's out of control, but not. I know that doesn't make any sense, but in my thought process, it does. It's like he can hurt people and it doesn't bother him, emotionally. I don't get it.

"Jokes are funny. Do you think this is funny?" The guy shakes his head violently in response to EJ's question.

"Tell him," Nik growls and shakes his victim a little more.

"He wasn't going to hurt her."

EJ gazes my way.

Hurt who? *Me?* I leave people alone. Why would anyone want to hurt me?

"She wanted Vinny to keep Keeley distracted so she could go after Nik and he told Vinny to get close to Keeley."

I gasp when EJ grabs the front of the snitch's shirt and lifts him off the ground. "She and he who?" When he doesn't answer right away, EJ shakes the guy.

Guilt floods my body. I caused this poor boy to get hurt. "Put him down. EJ, let's go." I suppose my earlier hurt and frustration toward Nik should be gone now that I know he's been out here fighting on my behalf, but it isn't. If he wouldn't have left in the first place... *No.* It's not his fault. It's mine. I never should have come to this party. Anger at myself for not listening to my own concerns zips through my body. "I'm leaving right now."

I turn. Using my hands to part the nosy teens, filming this shake down, I flee. As I push open the back gate and run to Etna.

Gratefully, EJ left the car unlocked. I collapse in the passenger seat of my car, the air suffocating me more than reality. I hit my hand against the dashboard, but life hit me harder. I would fight anyone who says anxiety isn't a chronic illness.

I need something to get hooked on, something to run through my veins and down my spine. A pleasure only headphones and a Shinedown song can give me.

15

THE STANDS ARE NEARLY empty, which is surprising for a Saturday afternoon game. I'm warming up with Cameron, Danny, and Kyle. Coach already gave Cameron the starting goalie position for today's game, so tensions are even higher as the darkness hidden behind last night's party looms.

"Keeley's not here yet?" Danny states the obvious in the form of a question thinking it would ease my nerves. It doesn't.

Her ghost played with my mind all night. Every minute that passed, I stared at the ceiling thinking of my unanswered texts. The one she did answer told me to give her space to work through this. How could I deny her that? *Because I wanted to fix it.* She's blaming herself for me roughing up that kid. Even Dion doesn't know who he is.

Coach is pacing up and down the field and venting. He heard about Vinny's charade last night and benched him. Vinny's parents fought with Coach Bucci and pulled Vinny off the team. This is what my grandmother calls the Twilight Zone. Who sticks up for their kid when he's the attacker, the bully? Apparently, Vinny's.

"We'll be alright without his presence on the field and that makes you Captain today." Danny's comments are grating on my nerves. The last thing I need right now is more responsibility.

No one seems to understand that. Even my dad continues to pressure me from behind bars to take his place in the mafia world. Keeley told me I was too rough on that kid last night. If she only knew… I could never do more than that. She has to know that I was protecting her.

Last night EJ dropped the semi-snitch and chased after Keeley. I say *semi* because he never did share who the "*she*" was that wanted me, or the "*he*" who bet Vinny to take advantage of my girl. When One Direction's line, *Everybody wants to steal my girl* rolls through my mind, I cringe. Being around Keeley again has influenced me a little too much. In retrospect, I haven't felt this alive since we were together in Italy.

"Get underneath that," Coach yells, already rushing the goal.

Poor Cameron. Being goalie is tough.

Two minutes until kick off. "What if Keeley doesn't show?" I ask Coach when he jogs toward me.

He glares at me for a second before he runs his hand through his hair. "I don't know." He turns away and it sounds like he mumbles, "Nothing is happening like it's supposed to."

"What was that?"

"Nothing."

"Captains, meet centerfield." I run when the referee calls.

After the coin toss, a rapid movement out of the corner of my mind steals my attention. Keeley. with EJ and her mom trailing behind.

I hope her dad isn't here. The last few days have been challenging enough, I don't need to deal with Mr. James and whatever his problem is with me.

I'd rather not think about Keeley's dad, or why EJ and Mrs. James give me a look of pity.

I reach out my hand to stop her. "Keeley, are you okay?"

She gives me a quick nod and keeps running—away from me.

No, no. no. I've spent the entire night beating myself up and questioning the events of last night's party. If I hadn't let her go in alone, none of this would have happened. Dion swears he didn't have anything to do with it, nor did he know who was behind the entire thing.

Someone knows.

I run after her, and gently pull her arm to a stop. "What's wrong?"

Tension and silence fill the space between us.

Her big green eyes gaze up at me. She's upset. "Truth?" she asks. I nod. "You hurt me, Nik." My heart drops. I know she's right, but telling her I didn't mean to seems stupid. "You knew I didn't want to come here and said you wouldn't leave me, but you did. I'm not saying it's your fault because you could have been sitting next to me and that could have happened if God wanted it to."

I raise my brows, almost questioning her rationale, not to mention her trust in me. "Please forgive me."

"There's nothing to forgive. You didn't do anything wrong. I'm just not in a good place." She crosses her arms over her chest.

I stifle my brows and extend my hand to her, hoping she'll lace her fingers with mine.

"I better not. My dad is here somewhere." I get it, but the rejection stings.

I nod. "Let me be here for you."

BERYL IS STARING AT Keeley and I as we reach the bench where Coach is already running through his, *non inspiring,* pregame speech. Was Beryl the *she* the kid was talking about? She has been sus lately being nasty one minute then tolerable the next.

She sashays over until she is shoulder to shoulder with Keeley. Her tone is snarky when she flips her ponytail over her shoulder. "If you're lucky, Coach will play you in the second half. He doesn't like it when players are late."

"Leave her alone, Beryl." I don't hesitate, interrupting Coach Bucci.

"Valentino, you know we have a game about to start, right?"

I cross my arms over my chest. "Yes, Coach," I say, not caring how annoyed my tone sounds. "Beryl is hassling Keeley."

"I'm fine." If Keeley's eyes shot daggers, I'd be dead.

Coach Bucci holds up his hand. "I know some of you experienced a horrible incident last night, but we have a soccer game to play and without Vinny we all need to step up."

"Where's Vinny?" Keeley asks.

"Coach kicked him off the team thanks to you," Emma snaps.

"That's not—" Coach Bucci barks.

"Thanks to me?" Emma smirks and nods her head. Keeley squares her shoulders off. "First of all, I didn't ask for anyone to do anything to Vinny. I'm not mad at him. He's obviously got problems acting that way. Secondly, I'm here to play soccer and I suggest anyone who isn't here to win should leave now."

That's my girl. Keeley's always been one to let people off the hook easily. It bothers me that she's forgiven Vinny already, but that's her. The only plus side is that I'm hopeful we'll be okay quickly, too.

"I've made a few changes to the starting line up."

Beryl whips around and smirks at Keeley. "I told you so," Beryl whispers. "Looks like you and I will be together again, Nik."

The way she says that with a flirtatious eye flutter, makes my skin crawl. Beryl's celebration is halted when Coach finishes his announcement— she is still riding the bench.

"Thanks for keeping the bench warm for us, Beryl." I say with a triumphant tone.

"That's not fair!" Beryl's indignant tone sounds more like a toddler's whining when she doesn't get her own way. "James was late today. Whenever a player is not here thirty minutes before a game you don't let them start."

"Not that I owe you an explanation, but James is the stronger player in this case..."

"In every case," I mumble, hoping she hears me, but I don't want to interrupt the best speech Coach has ever made.

Keeley bumps my arm. "Don't be wicked."

I lean closer and whisper into her hair, "I can't help being wicked hot." I kiss the top of her head. The corners of her lips curl quickly before she brings them back into the straight line—I've always called that her concentration look.

Moving into position, I say, "Maybe we can start our project tomorrow? You could come to my house after practice. I'm sure my grandparents would love to see you again."

"Really? I've only met them once. I'm surprised they'd remember me." I shrug like I haven't talked to them about Keeley for the last two years.

"It'll be fine. Okay?"

"Sure, but—" her words are cut off by the ref's whistle.

We line up for the kick off and the ball flies high in the air toward us. No one is saying anything as the ball descends from the air right in front of their players who snuck by me. Coach Bucci is clapping his hands and screaming. "What was that?!"

The center forward for The Sea Turtles struck quickly, and before we knew it, we were already down one to nothing.

I get why it got past me, with Keeley on my brain. But what happened to her?

The fans for the other team erupt into an obnoxious chant about being better. Whatever.

My lack of focus during the next play has the coach yelling at me for getting stripped of the ball, not once but twice. Then for dribbling the ball too far into the corner, allowing the defense to kick it out, and finally for missing the wide-open goal five feet in front of me.

I hang my head as I run to my position. I shrug it off, knowing beating myself up will only cause me to play even worse. With any luck we'll get the W and I'll finally get a mind-blowing kiss from my girl.

16

ONE CRUDE COMMENT MY dad projected across the field when I missed the opening of the game, awakened the soccer beast living within me.

What happened to the days when athletes hated (*maybe that's too strong of a word*)—disliked—each other, but when they stepped on the field they were teammates and worked toward a common goal—winning.

The goose egg on the scoreboard at the end of the first half screamed *loser*. Oh wait, that was my dad yelling at me in front of everyone, telling me to show up for the second half or don't bother to play.

"Hey, guys, you've got this. Your skills are superior to theirs, but you're letting them get in your head." My mom entered the conversation and my dad stood quietly listening to her just like my teammates and Coach Brent did. Then she dragged him away.

These people, I can't call them teammates because they aren't. They cared more about keeping the ball away from me than scoring the first half. No joke.

Now that the second half is underway, things are only slightly improved. When the final buzzer sounds, it's ten to six. Nik and I got three goals each in the last forty minutes. I should have changed my jersey. The other team passed me the ball more than my own. *Good grief.*

Certainly, losing is enough embarrassment for the afternoon, right? Wrong. Dad appears again without mom and blames Nik for keeping my head out of the game.

"Nik scored three goals, too, Dad. Eleven v. two are pretty tough odds, don'tcha think?

"Right, because you and Nikolaus are the only ones on the team." Beryl scoffs.

He ignores Beryl's comment to acknowledge mine. "You've got a point." My dad barely makes eye contact with me and then turns to Nik, continuing his rant. "I told you before to stay away from my daughter." Nik is nearly eye level with my dad. Adrenaline soars through my veins. He just told me to hang out with Nik when he wanted me to go to youth group. What the heck am I supposed to do? *Please don't fight.*

"We're teammates, Sir." Nik speaks calm and rationally compared to my dad's angry tantrum.

When my dad doesn't respond to Nik, but points a finger at me, inches from my face, I cringe. My hands shake and my stomach swirls with fear. Wiping my hands on my shorts, I clench them behind my back. I'm sure my knuckles are white. As he continues yelling at me, my brain shuts down, so does my hearing. It's like a silent movie and all I can see is his look of disgust and anger. The white noise changes to a ringing in my ears as my temples throb.

Nik steps forward and I cross my arm over my chest, using my bottom hand to create a stop sign. If he interjects himself, it will only make it worse. Thankfully, he stops, but I can see out of the corner of my eye that his hands are clenched into fists and the way he stares at my dad scares me.

"Alright, what's going on here?" Coach Bucci breaks up the growing crowd. "Oh, Mr. James, you must be proud of your daughter, scoring three of our six goals today."

My dad's hand drops, but he doesn't step back. "There's always room for improvement, right?"

Coach Bucci shrugs and nods as he dismisses everyone, but Dad doesn't wait. He's gone after he says his piece.

"Keeley, hang tight for a minute." Nik questions me with his eyes, but I nod, letting him know it's okay to leave.

Once it's the two of us, Coach Bucci, pulls a bottle from his pocket. "I know you are a better player than you're showing." He shoves the bottle into my unzipped bag. "Take one of those three times a day and you'll be ready for the scouts I have coming to look at you next week."

Scouts? I never planned on playing soccer beyond high school. I wasn't joking when I said I'd fly to Sicily to be with Nik. Now I might not have to. But, am I even good enough to play soccer in college? Probably not since Coach is telling me I need "assistance" to be better.

"Go on, get outta here." His command rips me back to the present.

It's bad enough we lost, but the walk of shame to the car nearly unraveled me. Was I that embarrassed by losing? Absolutely not. That happens when teams don't work together. I didn't expect to win, so why did my dad? Why did Coach Bucci think I needed something to give me the edge for scouts coming to visit? I guess the shame comes from being a disappointment. That is nothing new when it comes to my dad, but now Coach thinks I need drugs to play better. Not. Going. To. Happen.

I jam my AirPods in my ears and tap my music app. I chuckle to myself. How fitting—Simple plan.

As the song plays, my soul shrivels. I feel bad for the singer of this band, knowing how he feels. No one should have to grow up feeling like they're never enough for a parent. When I reach the parking lot, tears prick my eyes. Standing beside Etna are my mom and EJ. They stuck around for me. *I love them. Thank you, Lord.*

My mom doesn't wait; she jogs toward me and wraps her arms around my shoulders. Only a mom could handle how badly I smell after playing soccer for eighty minutes. Another verse plays in my ears while she hugs me.

She must've heard the song because she says, "Keeley, you always make me proud and you'll always be good enough for me." Tears form in my eyes; Mom always knows how to make me feel better.

What makes me the saddest? At least this singer remembers the days his dad spent with him. I can't. The only time he wants to spend time with me is to get information from me or put me down.

"You okay, sweetie. Well, I know you're not. Do you want to talk about it?"

"Not yet. Will you drive, so I can be the DJ," I ask with a smile.

"Anything for you, Beautiful."

My mom and EJ sing along with the music I choose, trying to pull me from my funk. Usually that works, but all I can think about is Nik's face when my dad embarrassed him. Why is he so angry about everything? Is something going on that he's not telling me, or is his anger stemming from me? I never thought of that before. I can't imagine turning Nik into that type of person. Maybe it's not a great idea for us to date.

And as much as I try to tell myself that I don't care that my dad doesn't like me, I hear my mom's words: *"If you're telling me you don't care, yet you're thinking about it enough that you care a little."*

Whenever I put myself out there to talk about music, he tells me that the music I listen to is garbage and only his music is great. Yeah, that is horrible, I know. But it gets worse. Multiple attempts later of listening to his music, I comment how I like a song from one of his bands. I expected a smile, or even better he'd turn on the music and we'd listen together. Nope. *"You shouldn't be listening to them. They aren't a great band."*

What?! Why is he listening to them then? *"I'm the parent. I don't answer to you."* We know what that means, don't we? No matter what I do, I lose. I'm wrong and I'm sick of it. So when am I going to stop caring, too?

"You did great, Keeley," EJ hollers over the music.

"Thanks, but apparently it's not only dad who thinks my performance needs a boost."

EJ laughs, clearly not hearing the second part of my statement. "I was concerned during the first play of the game that you might be too distracted with the Italian Dreamboat to play, but you came around."

I glare at him and he shrugs his shoulders as if to say, *I call it like I see it.* Even my mom is smiling.

"Mom!" She's supposed to be on my side.

She shrugs, too. *What the heck?* "He is very distracting, it's not your fault."

"Apparently, Coach feels like it's a bigger problem," I say again, but before either of them can ask what the coach said, I put my earbuds back in place, while I think about how I'm going to tell them I may have to quit the team.

17

RIGHT AFTER CHURCH ON Sunday I go for a run with Mom. The crisp afternoon air surrounds me, keeping me cool as the sun provides my warmth, and courage.

Being a teenager can really suck at times. We're told we're still kids, yet those same people expect us to act like adults. I pause for every teenager to cheer...loudly!

I have a great mom. So why does it feel like a Herculean task to tell her about what happened with Coach yesterday? It's embarrassing and I'm scared. Not that she'll be mad at me, but she'll be mad. Ever seen those mama bear videos on TikTok? Things don't end well.

The pills are still sitting at the bottom of my soccer bag like an anchor holding a yacht to the bottom of the Atlantic. Even worse, that same weight is an elephant on my chest, making each stride harder to push myself.

"Are you doing okay?" Mom asks me in between controlled breaths.

I slow to a brisk walk. "Not really."

"Wanna share? Or are you still processing?"

See? My mom is always mindful of my space. I usually feel bad, like I'm a nuisance to her, but she assures me I'm not.

"I need to tell you something, but you can't freak out and you have to let me handle it."

Her face tells me she is contemplating this. My mom is great at keeping my secrets, but when I tell her not to freak out, she usually does. Again, not at me, but she's ready to fight the world in my honor. It's sweet, but admittedly a little scary.

"I promise I won't freak out, but I don't promise I won't take action."

"Mom," I sigh, knowing that's the best I'll get.

"Take it or leave it."

I huff, holding back a smile, not wanting her to think I like her no nonsense personality.

"Fine." I take a deep breath and squeeze my eyes shut. I let the words rush out of my mouth before I lose my nerve. "CoachBucci-gavemepillsandtoldmeIhadtotakethem."

The narrow slit of my eye, peeking out from between my fingers, sees that I'm walking by myself. I stop and turn to find my mom staring at me. Her jaw, tight and her eyes murderous.

"Are you mad at me?" I question immediately, worry spurting from my tone.

She pulls me in for a tug. There's nothing like my Mama's hugs. Well, maybe Nik's, but that's another topic.

"I'm not mad at you. Thank you for coming to me. How do you want to handle this?"

She gently grabs my shoulders and pulls back so she can look at me. I shrug. "I'm obviously not going to take them, but if I get kicked off the soccer team—"

"Then you get kicked off the team. She throws her hands into the air.

I glare at her, wishing she didn't interrupt me.

"Sorry," Mom says and starts walking again, urging me to follow. I know her well enough that if she doesn't walk and let out the anger inside her, she'll explode.

"I don't want Coach giving drugs to someone else who might take them."

Mom's pace picks up basically into a slow jog. She's most definitely working through her "freak out" stage with speed walking. Her quietness is scary. Pretty soon I see her lips moving and whoever she's talking to in her head is getting a lashing.

"Who you talkin' to?"

She shakes her head. "Coach Bucci. Your father."

"You're not going to tell him, are you?" No, she wouldn't. If anyone knows how I feel about my dad, it's Mom.

I'm very impressed and concerned with how long it takes my mom to answer. If she tells my dad, then he'll blame me. I already hear his words infecting my thoughts. *"If you practiced harder... if you kept your head in the game... If you played with your heart... If you ate better foods..."*

Sadly, I'm sure he'll come up with more that I don't think of. That's because I am not mean and don't want to put others down. These phrases seem to be his favorites.

Mom likes to analyze things, too. She always tells me to think from whom and where comments come from to determine if they are worth taking to heart. I know he's a control freak who likes to manipulate things, so his words shouldn't matter, but he's supposed to be my dad, so it's hard and his words sting... a lot.

"I'll give you until Friday morning, then I'll take matters into my own hands."

"What are you going to do?" I blink, clearly not comfortable with my mom taking anything into her own hands.

"I'll be sure to tell you when I've figured it out, when the rational side of my brain returns. All I can promise is I won't be doing anything I'm thinking about right now."

I shake my head and laugh. My mother is great.

Regardless of what she does, I know my back will always be covered.

My phone vibrates in my pocket. "Uh!" I gasp after pulling it out and reading a text from Coach Bucci. Mom's looking at me with a concerned face. "Coach is making the team go to a ropes course on Monday instead of practice."

"That sounds like fun."

"I just want to play soccer." If the people on the team don't want to like me, I don't care. This may be high school, but I'm not here to make friends. I stopped trying a long time ago realizing my constant moving made it too hard when I did leave.

Case in point: Nik, who I just got a text from.

> **Italian Dreamboat: Did you see that we're going to a ropes course?**

I can hear the excitement and imagine him throwing his fist into the air.

> **Keeley: I wonder if it will be like the one in Sicily.**

Italian Dreamboat: No offense, but nothing here is like Sicily.

Keeley: Country snob!

Though, he's not wrong. I might apply for dual citizenship once I graduate. I don't know what I'm doing with my life yet, but one thing I know for dang sure: I won't be living anywhere near my dad.

"How's Nik doing?" my mom asks with a smile.

"What makes you think I'm texting Nik?"

"Your face is a beaming sun at noon."

One of the bad things about my mom is that she dissects every one of my facial expressions and knows what's going on in my head before I say anything.

"I take it Nik is excited for the ropes course?"

See?

I blush when my mother interrupts my thoughts. "Do you know what dad's problem is with him?"

She shakes her head. "If I did, I'd tell you. His mom was a lovely woman. I still can't believe she's gone. I feel bad for not keeping in touch," Mom says, with tears pooling in her eyes.

Keeping in touch must be something the entire Valentino family struggles with. Nik and I still haven't talked about the letters, and part of me wonders if I should even bother bringing it up.

The sun rises higher in the sky and I peel off my sweatshirt and wrap it around my waist. The leaves are trying to keep the Chlorophyll running through their veins, but they are slowly losing the fight.

Speaking of losing. My resolve to be upset with Nik is slowly slipping away. The way he wanted to step in and face off (yeah, I know, wrong sport) with my dad was romantic. I know he wouldn't have let me go in the house alone yesterday if he knew Vinny was going to attack me. So he must have a good explanation for not writing, too.

> **Italian Dreamboat: Do you wanna come over and work on our project**

> **We need to start soon**

We are almost home. "What's on the agenda for the day?" I am wondering, not so I can ditch her, because I like to help make the plans.

"Nik wants to see you, huh?"

I don't even have to ask. I can feel the heat creeping up my neck and into my face. It's important that we start our project; neither one of us would want to become ineligible if we didn't pass.

At some point in my musing, we arrive home and my mom makes a decision for both of us.

"We'll have lunch, then you should head to Nik's and... *study.*" Her smile and wink don't put me at ease.

"Mom!"

"Look, I'm not naïve. I know there will be more kissing than studying going on, but remember what I said..."

"*Spend a lot of time kissing. The unknown and anticipation is the best part. And all God wants until I'm married.*" I use a tone that could sound patronizing, so I apologize since I think she's right. But anticipation for a person with anxiety could also feel like a game of Russian Roulette.

I quickly text Nik, letting him know I'll be over after I eat and then, just as I expected, my anxiety flares. What would I give to be confident in my own skin? A kidney, maybe a hand—I don't need those for soccer. *Getting off track.*

I can only hope Nik and I are emotionally ready for this relationship and we don't ruin our friendship in the process.

18

NIK

THIS FEELS SO SURREAL. My gaze fixes on Keeley's profile. She's teasing me by tapping her pen against her lips. Then she holds it with her teeth to turn the page.

Not fair. She doesn't know what she's doing to me and I'm certainly not going to tell her. I have the urge to push her hair off her shoulder and let it cascade down her back, so I can get a better look at her flawless face. The thought has my heart pounding just a little quicker.

The tension is a thick, heavy blanket of unspoken and confusing thoughts... at least on my end. Keeley seems edgy or distant making it clear that I cannot bring up Friday night—the situation with Vinny or our almost kiss after we agreed we both wanted to date, or the soccer game.

"Stop staring at me. You're making me self-conscious."

Oops. Didn't mean to do that.

"Do I have to?"

Keeley slowly turns her head toward me and her gaze meets mine. In her usual casual tone she says, "I suppose I could blindfold you, but I'm hoping you'll just stop."

Blindfold? *Hmm.* I wonder if girls really can read guy's minds? I hope not.

"Sorry. Can we take a break and talk?" My buddies would say that I sound like a wuss, but I prefer the word vulnerable—thanks to my mom. After Keeley left Italy, my mother told me to stop moping around because she hadn't written. She brought me a piece of paper and pen. *"Be vulnerable. Tell her that you like her."*

I did. Keeley still didn't respond. I got the message loud and clear. *But now she's back.* And agreed to be my girlfriend, but she's acting like I'm still in the friendzone.

"Sure." Keeley's green eyes stare at me, challenging me to speak as she plops down onto her stomach. If I don't address this now we could slip back into simply being friends. No, thank you. But what if I say something and she's been intentionally avoiding it because she just got caught in the moment.

Why is this so awkward? *Because girls are scary.*

The battle going on in my head is nothing new, but now that we're so close, my heart and mind are on the brink of a civil war.

Now that I have her attention I need to say something. My palms are starting to sweat, and Keeley has raised her eyebrow more than once now. I hear her silent, yet, oh so loud questions: *Why aren't we working on this very important project? Can I help you with something? For the love of all things chocolate, say something.*

Yes, that's it! "Would you like some chocolate while we work on our propaganda poster?"

Her quick nod and bright smile lit up the room, making my heart skip a beat.

I'm off the bed and nearly at the door when she says my name. The softness of her voice melts me. I stop abruptly, place my hand on the door jam and turn back toward her. I didn't hear her moving, so when her body crashes with mine, my body instantly soars into an electrical frenzy.

She lets out a little "Oof," when her hands land on my chest. *Not helping! Space. I need space.* Teenage hormones are no joke, but I need to reign them in. With Keeley looking up at me with those ocean eyes, and biting on the side of her lip, she is sending a torrential wave of emotions throughout my body, and if I'm not careful that wave will come crashing down on me tsunami style.

She's the first to speak. "Do I make you nervous?" asking me the same question I asked her, on the first day I started walking her to her classes.

YES! You seriously have to ask me that? I huff out a quick breath of laughter. I've contemplated taking the door off the hinges to avoid any temptation to shut it.

"Why would you think that?" It's better to answer a question with a question when avoiding lying.

She smiles. "You're sweating and a little jumpy."

Besides the fact that I run hot anyway, her palms are searing my chest, and I fight the urge to pull her arms up around my neck, which will eliminate the inch of space between us. Her lingering hands make me wonder if it's intentional. I mean, she's well grounded—I have her by the waist. She never even came close to hitting the floor, yet, she's hanging on to me like I'm the last rock on the side of a cliff.

Definitely not complaining, I can't say any of this to her, but it would explain both of her observations.

"Are you nervous about working together since it's been so long?"

I rub my hand up her back since my body needs to move and I'm not about to move away. She'll have to create space if she wants it. "No, I wouldn't say that."

"Okay. What is it then? I'll tell you if you tell me." Her singsong voice brings me back to the time at the playground in Italy.

"Want me to push you higher?"

"Of course." Her laughter is brighter than the sun in the sky, and I feel a burst of happiness as it explodes in my chest. "Will you tell me what you got me for Christmas?"

"No!" She is so impatient.

"Aw, come on, you can tell me anything; we're best friends. I'll tell you what I got you, if you tell me."

Sure, I can tell you anything except that I like you more than a friend...

I didn't give in back then about the Christmas present or my feelings. But I've often wondered if things would be different now, if I had told her back then. I'm embarrassed to admit, if Keeley pushed me hard enough for anything now, I'd give her whatever she wanted.

Time seems to stand still as we gaze at each other. I wrap my arm around her waist even tighter, eliminating the space, while my other hand grips the wood beneath my fingers. You're supposed to ground yourself when an electrical storm lights up your world like nothing else, right? My lips are centimeters away from her forehead. Despite my distracting thoughts, I'm ready to get this conversation started, but she speaks first.

"Should we talk about our past before we get too far into dating?"

I don't acknowledge her question, I just blurt out mine. "Why didn't you write like you said you would? Every day I didn't hear back from you crushed me. I finally got one the night I left Italy, but I didn't even get to read it all before everything..."

Her hands fall from my chest, leaving an instant chill behind. If the slightly murderous look in her eyes and dropped jaw are any indication, I think she's mad.

"Me, not write to you?" Her tone is indignant. Her fists clench in an alternating pattern, which has me wondering if this conversation is going to hurt.

"I wrote you dozens of letters. All of them went unanswered, so I stopped. If I crushed you, then you decimated me in return."

She wins in the vocabulary department, but something is not right.

"Keeley," I say with the most tenderness I've ever heard come from my mouth. "I wrote you so many letters, but it wasn't until a year ago I received my first letter from you. My hand finally drops from the doorway and it cups her elbow, leading her back to the bed.

"You wrote me?" Tears pool in her eyes.

No, no, no. Don't cry. Yell, swear, heck pound on my chest if that takes the pain away, but don't cry.

"A lot." I rub my hands up and down her bare arms.

Her lips squeeze tight and she squints at me right before she lets her upper body fall back onto my bed. I lean back on my side, propped up on my elbow. This feels very intimate, but I place my hand on top of hers, which are resting on her ribs. "Talk to me."

"What did you tell me in your letters?"

I avoid her stare. "I told you how much I like you. It's even more now that we're together again."

"How are we going to date?" She props herself up on her elbows. "My father never lets us see one another? I mean EJ is the favorite. Dad played football and with EJ going all-state last year it's been worse. He can do no wrong, but with me…"

I wipe a rogue tear off her cheek with the tip of my finger. Turning her head toward me, she gives me a faint smile, which is absolutely beautiful. The more tears that stain her face, the more attractive she gets, to me anyway. It also makes me more angry with her dad. I'd do anything to protect her.

"He'll say sorry for uttering something stupid or thoughtless, but then he does it again. And…" she hops on her side, now our faces are mere inches apart. "He's like this with everyone. We have to walk on eggshells around him and then he blames us that he's upset. Really? I can't wait to turn eighteen and get out of there."

"What are your plans?" I feel bad asking her when I don't know my own. Uncle Sal keeps texting and calling, but I ignore him. A UPS driver has attempted to deliver three packages. I have no idea what's in them and I don't want to know. Every time I reject one, Sal reminds me of the family expectation.

The smirk on her face tells me it's something I may like.

"I planned on hopping a plane to the Mediterranean to find my best friend."

"Is that what we are? I recall dancing with a beautiful young woman who agreed to be my girl."

Keeley shakes her head. "I said that was what I've always wanted."

"Same difference." I wink. "I'm sorry things aren't good with your father. What if I tried to talk to him?" Her wide-eyed expression seems like a pretty hard no.

"What's that look for?"

She takes a deep breath and slowly and softly blows it out. "No one has ever stood up to my dad. You're either really brave, or really stupid."

Or option number three: I really like you!

If I lean forward slightly, our lips could meet for the first time. She parts her soft, full lips. That's an open invitation, no RSVP necessary, just show up, right? That's what my brain is telling me, but I still have unanswered questions.

"So you wrote me letters, too?" She grins and nods. "Did any of them write me off, or did they express your undying love for me?" Her rising blush tells me it's probably the second option. *Yes!* She tries to shove me away, but I don't let her. Instead I capture her wrist and press a gentle kiss against the inside, and I enjoy watching goosebumps form on her arms.

"I shared everything with you in those letters." She tucks her hair behind her ear. "I'm really embarrassed wondering who read them if you didn't."

She pauses long enough to get my blood spiking again, wondering what she put in those letters. I wait to see if she'll say more, but instead, my grandmother makes her presence known.

"Hey, would you like—" she abruptly stops in the doorway. "Oh, Keeley dear, what's wrong?"

It isn't hard to tell Keeley has been crying. Her usually bright face is surrounded by gray clouds threatening to drop a storm on her any minute.

My grandmother shoos me out of the way, nearly knocking me on the floor, so she can sit on the edge of my bed. She grabs Keeley's hand and covers their connected hands with her free one. "Did my grandson do something to upset you?"

"Me?! Seriously?"

That makes Keeley laugh. I guess, I don't mind my grandmother calling me out as the potential bad guy if it makes Keeley laugh.

"Can I tell her?" Keeley asks me, and for a reason I can't explain, that brings me so much happiness.

"Sure."

"Nik and I agreed to stay in touch with letters. All this time, I thought Nik didn't want to be friends because I didn't get any, but he wrote them."

"Same," I say from behind, but my grandmother is too focused on Keeley to pay attention to me. I can't say I blame her.

My grandmother pats Keeley's hand and stands, waving us to follow her out the door. "Come on. Let's have a snack. We can talk all about it and then you two can get *something* done on that project of yours."

Keeley and I glance at each other and smirk. We do need to work on our project. We've thrown ideas around, but we need to get drawing and writing before it's too late.

I gesture for Keeley to lead the way out and then nudge her shoulder. She stops without turning around and I wrap my arms around her. My chin rests nicely on her shoulder. The smell of orchids is invading my ability to think clearly. "We are not done with our conversation. I need to know where we stand."

Her breath hitches. When Keeley lets it out she says, "I stand with you."

I give her a quick kiss on the cheek before my grandmother beckons us. The smile on her face makes me more determined than ever to find out what happened to our letters.

19

NIK AND I STAYED up until the wee morning hours having what he called a text date. It's been nothing short of amazing reuniting with Nik, and learning of all the things I missed while we were apart, and I'm very worried about him. Something is sus about his family.

Now I'm dragging my butt around school, dreading practice today. "What does zip lining have to do with playing soccer?" I grumble, throwing my hand into the air.

"Settle down, Sparky. It'll be okay." Nik wraps me in a hug, nestling my shoulder against his chest—the best calming effect ever.

"Sparky?"

Nik rubs his hand on the back of his neck. "I figured you're a firecracker, so you can be my little Sparky."

"Aw, that's so—"

"Don't you dare say cute."

I button my lips, but can't hold it with my growing smile.

"Adorable," I blurt.

He shakes his head. "That's worse."

I shrug and giggle as if to say, *next time let me say cute.*

"I've never heard you giggle." Nik bops me on the nose with his finger.

"Me, giggle? I don't think so."

He shook his head. "You did, but it was so... cute. It wasn't the fake giggle girls use... it wasn't fake, right?"

"If I did giggle, no, it wasn't fake." I'm head over heels for you, Nikolaus Valentino.

"Good. Let's ride the wire then." He hands me the harness and I step each leg through a loop.

I gasp when his fingers brush against my bare skin, fire trailing his touch as he secures my harness. Another couple of inches and our lips could meet. A deep breath of his familiar ocean scent sends my desire to kiss him soaring.

"You alright. Is it too tight?"

I shake my head and stammer, "I-I'm good.."

"What's going on in that pretty little head of yours?" Nik asks while he fastens his harness.

It wouldn't be fair to burden him with my incessant thoughts of wanting to kiss him.

As if he can hear my thoughts, he hugs me. Our harnesses create the barrier between us that is totally necessary, at least for me. Sparks zing through my core when I notice his hands. They aren't just on my lower back; they are touching my skin. Either my sweatshirt hiked up when I reached around his neck to hug him, or more probably, he snuck his hand under the hem of my shirt. Either way, more skin to skin contact causes me to shudder. Breaking our hold, he studies me. "Are you sure you're okay?"

If by okay, you mean it's perfectly normal for a handsome guy like you to render me breathless, then yes, I'm absolutely fine... no problem.

His lips curl into a sly grin. "I take your breath away, huh?"

Again with the mind reading!

"Dream on." I shove his chest, but he holds me in place. The look he gives me sends a shiver down my spine as my breath freezes, hollowing out my belly.

For the first time in my life, I feel special, wanted... by the guy I've liked for years, who's now my boyfriend. But if he doesn't kiss me soon, I may have to take matters into my own hands.

Though countless scenarios race through my mind, like a frantic carousel of possibilities, I remain hypnotized by the burning intensity in Nik's unflinching stare. *Wow!*

"Hey Nik!" I peer over his shoulder to see who is mean enough to break my concentration, but Nik pulls me back, center with him. When the person calls him again, Nik laces his fingers with mine and guides me toward the tree line.

This may not seem like a big deal but to me, my heart leaps, anticipating what this secrecy means, and the sun is shining a lot brighter, or maybe it's the touch of Nik's hand branding every spot he touches: my hand, back, and now that we've stopped, my shoulders.

"We don't have a lot of time to talk, but we've danced around this," he gestures a finger back and forth between us, "long enough and I'm ready to move to the next step."

That's what I was waiting for, but now I'm rendered speechless. *Come on, speak.* "N-n-next step?" I heard him correctly, right?

He brushes his hand along my cheek and hooks his finger under my chin. "You'll always be my best friend, no matter what." his tender voice pulls me in; I'm hanging on every word, "but I want more."

A gasp catches in my throat, his words electrifying and unexpected, sending a surge of excitement through my body.

Still processing his words, I tell myself, *keep calm.* I fight the urge to jump up and down. *Don't overthink this.* The vibrant spark in his eyes mirrors the joy in me, making it easy to stare into his dreamy eyes. I hope I'm making him feel as wanted as he is me. Not that I could look away even if I wanted to when he stares at me like he never wants to let me go.

"You said you'd be my girlfriend and that you would stand with me, but you're being standoffish and unsure one minute then all girlie the next." He runs his hand through his hair. "I'm a guy. Take it easy on me, would ya?"

He cups my cheek, and I lean into his touch. "I want to be your girlfriend." I choke on my words. Still, a few baby nerves float around my belly amongst the excitement.

Nik smirks. "You'll have to say that again to make sure I heard you right."

"You heard me." I attempt to shove his chest, but he grasps my hand and kisses my knuckles.

"Is it so bad I want to hear it again?"

My stomach muscles constrict as I take a deep breath. I shake my head, hoping I don't pass out. It's my sincere hope that I'll hear my own voice again. *But if not, I'm sure I could find another use for my mouth,* I think as my gaze drops to his lips.

"Keeley..." his hand gently rests on the back of my neck, tilting it toward the sky just an inch. Our gazes are now locked. The vein in his neck pulses wildly, telling me that my heart isn't the only one fully invested. "Let's seal that with—"

"Valentino, James, get over here!" Coach barks, interrupting the moment.

We wave, acknowledging Coach without breaking our gaze.

"Say something, Keeley."

My hand travels up his forearm and I lean more into his hand. I open my mouth to speak, but it's desert dry and I quickly close it. With a slow exhale, I focus, trying to coax moisture back into my lips and my voice back into my throat. His eyes pleaded for me to say something soon.

Lord, please help. I swallow again and a slow smile spreads across my face.

"I've wanted this for years." His eyes widen, and my admission sends a panicking alert to my nervous system. I feel naked and vulnerable that something bad will happen, even though he literally just said he wants me to be his girlfriend.

His arms are around my waist, and my feet leave the ground. "It's official. Now I can hug you all I want," he murmurs against my hair and kisses me on the cheek before he sets me back down and we run off to join the group.

"Hi, I'm Brent and this is Joe. We own Adventure Park." They shake my hand like we're best buddies and he slaps Nik on the back and says, "How ya' doin', Nik?"

Confusion must have taken over my face because Nik explains, "Brent and his wife are my grandmother's neighbor."

After going over safety precautions and watching everyone hook and unhook our clips on the ropes, Brent tells us they have a team building activity for us. Once we are successful, we have the rest of the time to enjoy the ropes ourselves.

It doesn't take long to realize we aren't going to have much time for ourselves. Everyone is treating me, and Nik by association, like the black sheep of the team. Because of that, we failed the human knot, rope geometry, and the rope game.

While Brent and Joe are super supportive, Coach bellows at us the entire time. I notice the looks the two owners share with one another, as if they are questioning how we are a team at all, with Coach Bucci at the lead.

"It looks like you need to start working as a team, setting aside any feelings you have toward one another and work toward a common goal. It's apparent that won't happen today, so we're going to call it for now," Brent says diplomatically.

As everyone takes off their harnesses, Coach Bucci beckons me to the side where he questions me about the drugs.

"I'm not taking them. You can kick me off the team if you want..."

"This is so much bigger than that, Keeley." Coach is sweating and shifting from one foot to the other. Something is very wrong, but I'm not sure exactly what. Before I can ask any other questions, Nik interrupts us and Coach leaves. The two of us stay with Brent and Joe, to complete three ropes courses and ziplines. I overhear Nik cryptically talking with Brent about his dad.

I learned three things today. First, and it makes me smile the most, is that Nik is gentle with me and protective of me. Now, more than ever, I know that Coach Bucci is up to something bad, but I won't let him use me to get ahead. The last thing I learn is dreadful. Nik has secrets... They hover over us, weighing down my heart and mind. How will they affect our blooming relationship?

20

HAVING KEELEY BY MY side this week has been fantastic. Sunlight seems to pour from her warming my already warm body another ten degrees. I can tell she expects the worst when her anxiety flares, but I'll convince her she doesn't need to worry around me.

Coach Bucci has been near impossible to deal with since the ropes course. He's riding Keeley hard about everything. I can see he's ready to pounce when the girls at the end of the running pack join us for dynamic stretches.

"Glad you could join us, ladies."

I try to keep the rest of the team focused by counting out the stretches, but I'm fully invested in what he's saying to my girl.

Her eyes tell me I shouldn't be concerned, but I am. It's at that moment she unleashes on him.

"Well, if God wanted men's and women's bodies to work the same, He would have created our hips the same. I do think it's a shame that men's hips allow them to run like a well-oiled machine, while we slow women are only capable of growing little humans inside our hips."

And that's why I call her Sparky. I hide my chuckle with a cough. I'm so proud of my girl. She's usually able to refrain when it comes to adults being rude to her. Her dad has instilled being respectful to adults, however, she believes strongly that respect is earned, not given based on age.

Coach Bucci invades Kee's space, so I move closer. "I can see why people think you're a problem that needs to be dealt with."

What does he mean by that? What people? Her dad? Mr. Lee?

"Sprint another lap. That should make you out of breath enough to keep your mouth shut."

I sidle up to my girl. "That's enough. You're her coach; it's your job to encourage her and lift her up, not tear her down."

"Valentino, this doesn't involve you, so if you know what's good for you, you'll back off."

'Did her dad put you up to this. He's the only other person who doesn't respect her, yet demands respect from her."

"James, run. Valentino, lead the team, or I can find another captain."

Keeley softens her eyes. "Nik, forget it. Do your job."

For the next hour, Coach Bucci runs us hard; practicing goal shots and running drills. I feel for Keeley. Coach is running her dry. The floodlights illuminate the field, a sign that practice is over. "Quick scrimmage, set it up," Coach barks at us. *This is getting old.*

As captain, everyone is looking for me to take care of things. It's dèjá vu, reminding me of how my dad expects me to take care of things for him. Standing next to Coach Bucci, I cross my arms and ask, "Are you okay?"

"Valentino, don't involve yourself."

Right, like I'm not involved, since he's yelling at all of us. "Do you realize you're screaming at us?"

He turns and glares at me. "When you become an adult and have to deal with real problems, then you can criticize me. We have a game tomorrow, and none of you are ready."

Hot, prickly anger rises within me, a pressure building in my chest. I search the field for Keeley. When I find her, her smile slowly fades, replaced by a look of worry as she takes in my expression.

But there isn't any time to talk. Coach is ranting, "Scrimmage, let's go, or I'll find a whole new team of players who actually want to play."

"He certainly won't be nominated for a motivational speaker award anytime soon," Keeley whispers as she jogs past me.

I chuckle in agreement.

My uncharacteristic reference to information I've learned in history gets me a wink. She is the most beautiful girl I've ever seen, and she winked at me! I can't lie. My heart is soaring.

After I get my head in the scrimmage, I score twice before Coach calls it a night. For everyone except Keeley. Her expression is pained as he waits for the field to clear to talk with her.

I linger as long as I can, pretending to load my backpack.

"Hurry up, Valentino. Get on outta here."

I stand up, crossing my arms over my chest, wishing I had thought of something to say that would force me to stay behind. Does it surprise me that I don't have any answers? *No.*

Lately, my only thoughts are on Keeley.

"I'm pretty sure James can take care of this on her own." Coach nods his head toward the parking lot.

Reluctantly, I throw my bag over my shoulder. "Is that right, Keeley, or do you want me to stick around?"

Her expression softens as she gives me a barely there nod. I respect her wanting to handle whatever this is on her own, but I can't give Coach the satisfaction of sending me away. I stop next to them and *accidentally* knock Coach with my bag when I lean down slightly and kiss the top of her head. Then, I say, "I'll call you later," before I glance back at Coach Bucci.

I get it. He's there to critique us and he's usually spot on, but lately, he's changed. For one thing, he's not critiquing us. I haven't heard him tell one player what they needed to do to improve; I've only heard him belittle us and yell.

Once I reach my truck, I throw my bag in the back seat and slam the door a little harder than necessary. Yes, I'm angry. I try to put all the blame on Coach Bucci, but I'm mad at myself, too. I shouldn't have left her there. Doubt ripples through me.

I turn and take one last look on the field. They are still talking. It's about time I put my plan into action.

⚽⚽⚽

KEELEY ISN'T ANSWERING HER phone or responding to my text. Worry fills my gut. Coach has been off, but he wouldn't hurt her, right? I text EJ, but he confirms that he saw her at school when he left with a buddy after his practice. She wouldn't still be there an hour after practice, would she?

As I pull into the school parking lot, Etna looks lonely. Floodlights illuminate the field and I see Keeley driving soccer ball after soccer ball into the net.

I grab my surprise for her and rush onto the field. *Maybe I shouldn't have left her,* I tell myself, feeling disappointed I let Coach Bucci push me around.

With my gift for her behind my back as I approach, she doesn't even make eye contact with me.

"Three more shots," she tells me. She pounds one ball into the net. "Why am I not enough for anyone the way I am?"

You're more than enough for me, I think, but she doesn't look like she wants an answer, so I keep quiet.

Keeley wails on the next ball and it gets caught under the net. "If I'm so bad, why isn't anyone helping me instead of criticizing me?" The last ball sails over the top of the net, into the woods.

"I'll grab that," I say while jogging off.

My gaze skims over the field as I return the ball swiftly. With her back to me, Keeley is putting the balls in the bag. Thankfully, she's done for the evening. Maybe I can get her to tell me what happened, but not before I try to make her day a little brighter.

I'm not sure this is the best time, but it's all I've got. I remind myself to breathe and wrap an arm around her waist, not caring that she is a poster child for a sweaty athlete right now, but I'm definitely not telling her that, or that I think it's kinda hot.

Her entire body is tense, so I just hold her, pulling her closer to my chest, hoping she'll relax a little. I make a mental note to talk to Grayson about Coach Bucci. Since his mom is also the Athletic Director, hopefully she can do something about the coaching situation.

I drape my other arm over her shoulder, placing a single rose in her vision.

She sinks against my chest. I can't recall a time that I wasn't playing soccer when my heart beat this fast. I'd like to blame it all on my nerves, anticipating Keeley's response to the question I've rehearsed all day. But worry and concern for her well-being took over a long time ago. It also doesn't help that I have this beautiful girl in my arms. Something better give, or I might have a heart attack.

"What's this for?" Keeley's soft voice encourages me to speak.

I kiss her on the cheek, knowing that my earlier idea of sealing this moment with our first real kiss, sadly, isn't going to happen. Not with her upset. I've waited this long. It won't kill me to wait a little longer for the perfect moment.

"For you. I am hoping you'll be my homecoming date."

Her fingertips gently capture the stem. Our fingers brush and I feel the tingling through my arm. The sensation reminds me of something my mom told me.

"When touching a girl's hand makes your sting, hold on to her. That's God's way of telling you she's probably the one for you."

Mom's past words cut deep. She'd always trusted in God. I deserted him when she died. He'd never forgive me for that, would he?

"I'd love to be your date; that'll be our first outing as a couple." Keeley's smile lights up the semi-dark parking lot. I turn her around and squeeze her against my chest, unable to resist being close to her.

I whisper close to her ear. "Thank you." Her sweet giggle vibrates in my chest. Man, this girl is adorable.

"I hate to ruin this moment, but will you tell me what happened with Coach?"

She stiffens again.

Okay. This is definitely a hot topic issue. Walking along the black sand around Mount Etna seems like it would be easier to traverse than diving into whatever happened.

Keeley squeezes me harder, like I'm a lifeline. Oh, there is no way I will drop this subject now. The longer she avoids the situation, the worse it will get.

"If you don't want to talk about it now, that's fine... But I'm not letting you leave until you tell me what's upsetting you."

My body isn't prepared for the way Keeley leans back and stares up at me with her big green ocean eyes. They call to me like the ocean itself, pulling me into the depths of her soul.

"Please..." I'm not above begging when it comes to making sure Keeley is okay.

21

"THANKS FOR TAKING ME to get my dress, Mom," I say, flipping through the gowns on the rack.

"Are you kidding? I am so excited to do it. I'll do your hair in that bridal twist with side braids you've always liked, if you want.

I pull a dress off the rack and drape it over my arm with the others I will try on. "That would be awesome. Thank you,"

With an arm load, I head to the dressing room while mom stands just outside the door. She isn't out on her phone in the waiting area like the other moms.

"Tell me what's going on with Nik, if you don't mind."

A giggle escapes before I can catch it. I've decided giggling isn't bad as long as it's authentic.

"That good, huh?

I put on the first dress. It's an off the shoulder sky blue dress. "It matches the nail polish Nik used to paint my nails. What guy does that?"

Mom agrees. "That's the sweetest thing I've ever heard."

"I know right." I say, opening the door to show mom the dress that I'm not quite feeling.

Mom smiles. "You are gorgeous, but something's off. Try on the second one," she says, after studying me, and asking me to turn around.

The girl next to me calls her mom to look and she brushes off the girl telling her, "I'm sure you look great in anything, just hurry up, so we can get home."

My heart is sad for that girl.

Thirty minutes later, with my mom's help, I selected the perfect dress. The full-length, maroon formal dress has spaghetti straps and layers of tulle that makes me feel like a princess. The silver, sparkly rhinestones on the bodice shine.

I open the door and my mom gasps. "You'll be picking Nik's jaw up off the floor when he sees you."

"Is dad grumpy about me going?"

"No. He's a smart man, so whatever you do, keep a strong moral compass and don't lie to him."

I huff. "I don't lie."

"Whoa. Let me start over." Mom takes a breath. "He knows you're going. If he asks you about going with Nik, don't get nervous and clam up or be tempted to lie, though I know you wouldn't, because he's Navy intelligence for a reason."

"Okay. But you trust me, right."

Mom shakes her head. "Yes, of course, I do. I'm just saying you could choose to talk to him about going to homecoming with Nik instead of leaving the house with your brother. It could bring you guys closer."

"Doubtful."

I'm not willing to take the chance that Dad pulls Nik and I apart again. Not when I'm finally happy. Doesn't he have enough trouble throughout America and the rest of the world he's trying to combat? Is another battle on the homefront what he's looking for? I won't surrender, so if he fights me, this will be his toughest battle to date.

22

THE RELENTLESS PRESSURE OF the past few weeks is catching up with me. A storm of frustration and resentment toward Coach Bucci and my dad thunder through my mind.

Who does Coach Bucci think he is? He can't give performance-enhancing drugs to players. This is high school soccer. Vice Principal Johnson has done nothing since I stopped at Grayson's house the night Keeley told me and I ratted Coach out.

As often as humanly possible, I push thoughts of my dad away. What can he do from behind bars? A lot. I've found out the hard way. He sent another package; I declined it. Once the delivery driver left with the package, I washed my hands of it. Or so I thought.

The driver returned one day when my grandmother was home. She saw it addressed to me and didn't question it. Instead, she left it on the counter and I promptly put it under my bed when I got home. I have to get it out of here. My grandparents shouldn't have to deal with this. They've already given up their retirement life to raise me.

They've never shown me anything except love and I'm just trying not to let my father mess with their lives like he is mine.

It's the second week in October and the temperature drop from the mid sixties down to forty is harsh—lung altering—when trying to push the limits during eighty minutes of play time. Principal Williams wasn't kidding when he said the school didn't have enough students to play.

That's why I'm spending my evening outside with my soccer ball. With Coach's perpetual bad mood, I'm afraid he might bench me like he did Keeley if I make a minor mistake. I think he did it to make a point about the drugs, but I can't prove that. Mr. James let him know that if he ever benched Keeley again, he'd regret it. I don't know exactly what Mr. James does in the Navy, but I'm smart enough to know that I don't want to find out...or ever be on his bad side.

I chuckle since I believe I already am on his bad side. So much so that EJ has to drop Keeley off at my house for homecoming and then go pick up his date.

"Ow!" I kick the ball into my rebounder and it sails back in my direction with the force of an atomic bomb nailing me in the gut. Apparently, I don't know my own strength because my next kick sends the ball over the fence into the neighbor's yard. A little scream from the other side has me running toward the gate.

"Andrea, are you okay?"

Her voice goes quiet and I fumble with the lock on the gate, hoping she is okay. She was in a wheelchair after a horrific accident that stole her parents from her. Since then she's had multiple procedures and surgeries and is able to walk, but she still has her chair for times when her body gets tired. I can't imagine the damage I might have done if she couldn't get out of the way quick enough.

Finally! I push open the gate and explode into her backyard. With a few more weeks left in his season, Brent is still at Adventure Park. My grandparents and me for the past year have been the support she or her kiddos might need while Brent is away, which is why Brent installed the gate in the backyard.

For a fraction of the second, I scan her backyard, squinting to spot her, though the twilight makes it a challenge.

"Andrea? Are you okay? Where are you?"

I'm not completely surprised when she appears from behind the bushes, tossing my soccer ball at me. Both her and Brent aren't as old as my parents, but they are parents and it's been refreshing to talk with them about... Everything from my mom's death, which sadly, Andrea relates to well, soccer, and Keeley.

Brent, popping out with her, does surprise me and I jump. "I'm really sorry. I guess I let my frustration out a little too much... I didn't hurt you or break anything, did I?"

I love living next door to them, but if I'd broken anything, Brent would have made me work it off at Adventure Park or made me his right hand man at youth group the next time.

"Don't worry about it," Brent fist bumps me and gestures toward the pool. "We can chat while the kids sleep, if you want."

I look at my watch. It's only seven. They must have heard my thoughts. Andrea laughs, "Daylight savings is a killer at first. I'll pay for it in the morning, don't worry."

For the next twenty minutes, I tell them about the threat my dad put on Keeley weeks ago and my desire to protect her. Aside from the packages—one's I haven't told them about—he's been silent since. For some reason, I find that a scarier concept than if he harassed me daily.

I exhale a deep breath and blurt out the current issues with Coach.

"I knew I didn't like that guy." Brent shoves his hand through his hair. "Ya know, he tried to take the youth group from us."

"As if."

Andrea claps her hands together and hops in her seat. "Do you know what color dress she's wearing, so you can coordinate your tie?" She pauses while Brent and I share a look. "Oh, you have to take her to Guido's first. That's so romantic."

I've heard the story of how their best friends Joe and Donna, who are equally lit, set them up on a double date at Guido's when they first met.

Brent slowly turns his attention to his wife. With a grin he says, "That's what you got out of everything he said?"

Her empathic eyes met mine. "I'm so sorry. You're right. I was just hoping to focus on the best part of what you told me."

I bite back a laugh. I can see why Brent looks at his wife like she hung the moon. She is an inspiration to everyone she comes into contact with.

"When's your next game?" Brent asks, refocusing on the issue with Coach Bucci?

"Tomorrow at 4:30." The intensity in Brent's voice and eyes has me wondering about his plan.

He pulls out his phone and taps on his screen. "Joe and I will be there."

"You don't have to do that."

"I know. I want to."

I can tell by his tone that he is not burdened by this at all. The joy bubbling inside me has everything to do with this man, my grandparent's neighbor, treating me like his son, and coming to my rescue.

23

NIK

I SPEND THE ENTIRE warm-up amped up. Keeley got called to the principal's office right as we headed to the locker rooms. This isn't how our version of the homecoming game is supposed to go.

Of course, the football team gets the highlight game tomorrow night before the dance on Saturday, but this is a big deal for us soccer players.

Sadly, Vinny is lurking around; his presence, threatening to make this the worst game of the season. I'd really like to check on Keeley, but I wouldn't mind putting Vinny in his place either.

"You got this, Nik!" I turn toward the sideline where Andrea and Brent are setting up their folding chairs next to Joe and Donna's. All four wave back at me when I acknowledge them, chuckling when I hear Joe yell, "Nik is the G.O.A.T." I laugh even harder and shake my head when Donna says, "Stop, you'll embarrass him."

Grayson and I warm up next to Kyle and Dion.

"Did you hear about Coach?" Dion tries to whisper, but the wind whisks his voice well across the field, forcing Coach Bucci's head to pop up in our direction.

"Less talk, boys, and more practice," Coach growls.

Oh, I'm not interested in warming up even though I know this is a very important game—without this win, we won't make it to the playoffs.

"So," I say, passing the ball back to Grayson. "What do you know?"

Before he can answer, Kyle mutters, "Watch out."

The warning is a little too late. Mr. James grabs me by the arm and whips me toward him.

The universe seems to hate me. I don't have the energy to deal with Keeley's dad.

"Where's my daughter?"

I cross my arms to appear bigger. My muscles speak for themselves, or so Keeley says, but her dad... I don't feel like dying today.

Don't laugh. I press my lips together.

The way he eyes my stance tells me he already knows he's intimidating. Is this why Keeley hasn't dated? If so, I should befriend the man snarling in front of me. We could be a great team, keeping Keeley safe.

"Dude, say something," Kyle whisper yells from behind me, breaking me from the array of thoughts that run through my mind.

Mrs. James appears by his side with concern etched on her face. Thankfully, before I have to tell them she's with the Vice Principal, I see Grayson's mom and Keeley walking side by side out of the building.

"There she is."

Mrs. James releases a heavy breath only to gasp again when three police officers are trailing them... And Vinny. When did he leave the field? Why is he with them?

Didn't see any of that coming.

I barely contain a gasp. True to form, Mr. James whips back in my direction, pointing his finger in my face, blaming me for whatever is happening.

"Your father is going to bring you down with him. Is that what you want?"

Clearly that was rhetorical because he continues with his rant, using his commanding Navy voice. A quick glance at Keeley's mom and I see her smiling.

I thought she liked me. I can't imagine why she thinks her husband's show is anything to grin at.

"Let me tell you something..." Mr. James growls as he steps forward, forcing me backwards, away from everyone. I am grateful for that when he speaks again. "I don't want you near my daughter because your father is a mafia boss."

"Derrick! Now is not the time or place!" Mrs. James scolds her husband with her eyes.

How awkward. Pretty sure everyone on the sidelines is watching, but I hope no one hears. If Keeley finds out before I can tell her, she'll never trust me.

Brent and Joe are on their feet studying this showdown, like they are ready to intervene if necessary. They aren't as intimidating as Mr. James, but I wouldn't mess with either of them.

"Thank you, Mrs. James, but he's correct." Focusing on her, hoping to erase the alarm pooling in her eyes, I say, "My dad was arrested about a year ago. The same day my mom died."

"Hmmm." Mr. James rests one arm across his chest, propping up his other arm under his elbow, resting his palm against his jaw.

With the speculation on Keeley's dad's face, I don't have time to ponder this. The police are approaching fast, and I need Keeley's parents to know I'm nothing like my dad.

"I'm grateful the Sicilian government wouldn't let my Uncle Sal raise me like my dad wanted. They ushered me here to live with my grandparents that night. No matter what he's asked me to do, I refuse."

Mr. James's hands drop. "Have you contacted your dad since his arrest?"

Without thinking, I nod. I've never admitted this to anyone. Despite his scary demeanor, I have a feeling of protection as it washes over me. Not that he cares if something happens to me, but maybe Keeley.

"We need to chat after this game. It's serious, Son."

Son? Who is this man kidding? He doesn't think of me as a son any more than he thinks of Keeley as a daughter—from what she says, anyway. What could he possibly want from me?

Keeley's gaze locks with mine. She looks relieved. Vinny keeps a respectable distance behind Keeley, and her mom is smiling. What the heck?

"I'm proud of you." Mrs. James whispers loud enough for Keeley to hear, which means her husband and I hear, too.

"What's going on, "Michelle?" The commander doesn't sound very pleased with his wife at the moment, so I am thrilled when Vice Principal Johnson asks us to follow her to the bench.

Brent and Joe run to join us.

"Hello, Vice Principal Johnson," Brent says, keeping pace with the group. "We're joining as parental guidance for Nik."

"That's fine as long as you don't get in our way," one officer says, pulling his shoulders back so his chest moves higher in the air.

As we approach Coach Bucci, the man is pacing back and forth, sweating bullets. If this were the beginning of the season under the scorching August sun, I'd get it. But in the dark October afternoon? No. I need gloves to keep my fingers from turning into popsicles.

"Keeley, what's going on? I was worried you wouldn't make the game." Coach's voice cracks like a cool canning jar in boiling hot water.

This is sus! Coach never calls her Keeley.

His eyes dart from Keeley's dad—understandably—to Mrs. Johnson and then to the police. His confused expression might be believable if he hadn't been acting strange the past couple of weeks. Coach looks at Brent and then Joe as he asks, "Who are you two?"

"We're here for Nik," Brent says.

Guys don't cry, I tell myself. My dad has always "taken care of me" in a *I have a lot of money I can throw at you to keep you busy and out of my way.* Never has a man been there to stick up for me.

"Mr. Bucci," the officer to my left begins. "Where did these come from?" He holds up a pill bottle.

"I-I...uh, why are you asking me? They're not mine."

Sure. I almost chuckle at the cliché, but considering the dire situation, I refrain. The officers have to know he's guilty. The profuse sweating alone is enough of a clue, but his little step touch back and forth could make me sick if I was prone to motion sickness.

"So you're denying the allegations that you gave these drugs to Keeley James, telling her, and I quote, 'You need to take these or you'll go nowhere in this life.'"

"That's absurd." Coach says as he traps his shaking hands underneath his armpits. I didn't miss that, and based on the shared look among the officers, neither did they.

The stern officer who put Brent in his place earlier speaks in a fierce, deep voice. "This is your chance to tell your side of things. It might get you out of the quicksand you are slowly sinking in."

"This is all his fault!" Coach yells as he extends his arm and points his finger in my direction.

Why does everyone keep blaming me? Before I can say anything, Mr. James speaks up first. "How is he responsible for you giving my daughter drugs?"

He steps forward, and all the officers follow suit. If I didn't know better, I'd think Keeley's dad was sticking up for me. Since the man hates me, I know that's not the case, but it felt nice for a minute.

I am still waiting for Coach to answer the question when Vinny speaks up. "This isn't Nik's fault and you know it."

What?!

Vinny looks sincere when he says, "I'm sorry, man. He told me I had to—"

"He's lying, too. Nik, you and Keeley are off the team. I can't have players I don't trust," Coach Bucci yells, grappling for control that's slowly slipping away from him.

"Mr. Bucci. That is no longer your concern," Mrs. Johnson declares, using her principal voice. She pulls out her phone and taps the screen. Coach's voice is loud and clear, telling Keeley she needs to take the pills and her refusal is just as crisp.

"He'll kill me and my family—"

Grayson's mom stops the recording and stuffs the phone into her pocket. "You are no longer an employee here. Officers, he's all yours."

They moved forward. "You have the right to remain silent..."

As they read him his rights, I can't help but stare. Is he afraid of my dad killing him and his family? I hope not. He may be a jerk, but I don't want to see him dead.

I'm still confused about how this all unfolded, but Keeley is in her mom's arms. An ache in my chest thumps, wishing she was in my arms right now. Do I offer?

I don't get the chance.

Officers lead Coach away. He glares at me. "You've dug your own grave. Why take everyone down with you?"

Really? Still blaming me because you tried to drug Keeley and who knows what Vinny was referring to?

"Come on, let's go." The officers tug him away.

Mr. James wraps his arms around his daughter and wife, but glares at me. "What are you involved in?"

"Dad, leave him alone. Nik is a good guy. You don't even know him."

"With all due respect, Mr. James," Brent adds, "Nik is a solid kid."

"With a dad in the mafia."

I can't meet Keeley's gaze, but I'll hear her gasp for weeks. I shift from foot to foot, mirroring Coach Bucci moments ago.

Yes, I'm nervous. Who wouldn't be?

"I'm not—"

"Getting anywhere near my daughter." Keeley's dad cuts me off, scowling at me like I'm next in line to take over.

Wait, I am.

But I've declined. That has to count for something.

"I don't know what's going on," Brent speaks with an even tone, "but we need to let Nik explain."

Tell the truth. You haven't done anything wrong.

I briefly recount the night my mom died, and how the authorities sent me to live with my grandparents. "It's not the life I want for myself or my future kids, so I keep telling him no."

"I get it, Nik. You were scared. You still should have told someone to help you." The tenderness in Keeley's mom's voice reminds me of my mom.

I know. Would anyone have believed me that I wasn't trying to bring the Sicilian Mafia to the little town of Eastland, Maine?

"You and I need to have a conversation." Keeley's dad demands.

Brent focuses his attention on me. "If you want me with you, just say the word."

"Me, too." Keeley stands straight up.

I know how rocky her relationship is with her dad, but she's willing to buck heads with him...for me.

My heart is thumping against my ribs. There are so many questions ricocheting around my head.

But for the first time since I've known this family, I feel that Mr. James doesn't hate me. Maybe it's too early to announce I'm taking his daughter to homecoming in two days, but he seems willing to listen to my full story, and possibly help.

What will he say when he finds out I have boxes from my dad, containing *whatever* under my bed? Just so there aren't any surprises, I tell him as much.

"Will you come to my house? I have to show you something that is probably really important."

He nods.

"What about the game, Mrs. Johnson?"

No surprise Vinny is asking about the game. Will his parents allow him back on the team? Until I know his entire involvement...

Vinny's parents rush to join the group. "Keeley, thank you for being such a forgiving person. We hope Vincent has apologized to you again. We're sorry for everything that happened." Vinny's dad steps forward and shakes Mr. James's hand.

"Vinny, you have Keeley to thank for being back on the team," Grayson's mom begins.

My head whips in her direction, and she shrugs.

"What did I miss?" I ask, as a sour feeling in my stomach threatens to make an appearance.

"As long as you promise not to drink, you're welcomed back."

"Thank you. Keeley. I am really sorry. Coach promised me a lot of money my parents could use since my dad's company is downsizing and...it doesn't matter. I was wrong and I'm truly sorry." She smiles at him and nods.

"Is there a coach over here?" The head referee joins our group.

Mrs. Johnson flashes her principal smile. "We've run into an issue, but we'll have a coach in a few minutes."

They walk away, seemingly satisfied with her answer.

"Joe and I are happy to take over for the rest of the season if you need us to." Brent offers like it's the most natural thing in the world.

"I believe you were player of the year for your *football team*, right? What do you know about soccer?" Mrs. Johnson asks.

"Well," he says, crossing his arms over his chest, "those were my high school days. There aren't many football leagues for guys our age, but there are soccer ones, and we've been playing for a few years now."

"I think it's a great idea," Mr. James offers. "You kids do your best to forget this and go win the game and extend your season.

24

"I'M DONE. THAT'S IT," EJ exclaims after Mom takes a photo blitz on her phone of the two of us dressed up for homecoming.

"Fine," she says reluctantly, putting her phone back in her pocket.

The moment Dad steps into the room, a heavy, suffocating tension fills the air.

"Have a nice time at the dance you two." Dad arches his brow and flexes his crossed arms so I can see his muscles move.

Why are men so weird?

He's staring at me as I make my way to the door, causing my heart to race wildly in my chest. Thumping extra hard at moments such as these, as if it's trying to escape my body.

Does he know? Is it wrong that I want to tell him?

Though a tiny voice urges me to share my life with him, to seek his guidance and learn from his experiences, he's never been a safe person to talk to.

As much as I love the idea of my thoughts, it's just too risky. He'll share the ideas that I talk about with people who gossip, or he'll dismiss the topics entirely, and he might even betray the way I feel about something. When he gets that upset, he ignores me, making my anxiety spike even further. So, it's better if I avoid anything other than a surface level relationship with him.

I catch mom's wink, telling me he probably does know. She knows how to talk with him, so she probably told him.

Why isn't he stopping me, putting his foot down? My guard is lit up like a prison yard looking for escapees.

"Make sure you take care of her tonight," Dad says to our backs.

A half-chuckle burst from EJ's lungs. "I stand a better chance of needing someone to take care of me tonight than she does."

Aw, that girl better not turnout to be more like Trish than she's shown thus far. I'll have to teach her a lesson if she hurts my brother.

"I'm there for you, bro," I assure him, placing my hand on his shoulder.

"Both of you be safe," Dad says as I make direct eye contact with him and my mouth goes dry.

⚽⚽⚽

"You look..." Nik doesn't finish his sentence, causing the anxiety in my gut to swirl. The heat in his eyes locks me in place. I bunch the maroon tulle at my hips between my fingers.

The closer he moves, the harder my heart pounds. He has to hear it.

Nik opens the passenger side door and cups my elbow, helping into his truck. "Sorry, I should have asked my grandpa to use his car."

"Don't be sorry. I like your truck." And your hand on my elbow. *Oh, and now my lower back.*

He jogs around the front of his truck; the lights shining on his dark gray suit and maroon tie that matches my dress color.

"Hubba, Hubba," as my mom said when she watched Thor for the first time.

He settles in the driver's seat, and he's staring at me. My pulse is racing and my stomach twists in knots. I bite the side of my lip. *Great! I probably have lip gloss on my teeth now.*

"Keeley," he says, but stops. I assume he's waiting for me to look at him. Our gaze meets. His eyes are dark and intense.

"You are absolutely stunning."

"Thank you." I say and break the way-to-intense-eye contact between us.

I finger the layers of my dress. "You're..." *My hot Italian Dreamboat,* I think silently before finishing. "dashing."

He chuckles and pulls out a plastic container housing a Taylor Swift red flower. I grin, watching him pry the tight corners open.

"What? I swear they make these hard to get into just to make us guys look inept."

Inept? Stunning? He's pulling out all the stops tonight. What am I talking about? I've never paid attention to his vocabulary before. I know he's intelligent. My rattled nerves make me believe that focusing on him will set things right.

The corners break free, and the corsage is airborne. We both reach for it, but his reflexes are a split second quicker. Our hands collide and like the champ he is, he has my fingers resting in his palm and the corsage is dangling from his pointer finger on his other hand.

"I'm sorry," I say.

For what? Not catching it? Hitting his hand? Him buying it? That we're heading to the dance? I don't have the slightest clue what I am apologizing for and thankfully, in true Nik fashion, he doesn't call me out either.

Once he slides the elastic on my wrist, he kisses the back of my hand and then shifts his truck into gear.

"It's gorgeous, Nik," I say as I study the flower on my wrist.

"Remember when you made confessions to me on our Mount Etna hike? Your second confession was that you had a crush on a boy, but was worried he wouldn't like you."

I will not admit that the boy I was speaking about then was him.

"I vaguely remember something like that."

He lets out a half laugh. "Mmmhmm."

"What?" We're both laughing as we pull into the school parking lot. He shuts off the engine and turns in his seat.

"Who was the boy, Keeley?"

His question should not have my pulse racing, but it does. It should not have my palms starting to sweat—ew—but they are.

He slides closer and brushes a strand of hair away from my eye and lifts my chin with his finger. "You trust me, right?"

Yeah. Even though I still don't know all the details around his mafia family, I do trust him. But what happens if my dad finds out information that would make me not trust Nik? Before my mind spirals into a twister of anxious thoughts, Nik squeezes my hand.

"I do." With courage not of my own, I look him in the eyes. "Nik, you know the boy I had a crush on was you."

A slow grin fills his face, warming me from the inside out. "I'd hoped so. Has my girl's crush grown stronger?" he asks, leaning closer.

"Has it been a slow week? Are you fishing for compliments?"

He let out a hearty laugh, then sobers. "You've become so shy around me; I miss my blunt girl."

"My feelings are far beyond a crush," she reveals. He leans over the console slowly. I find myself leaning, too. We are finally going to have our first kiss. His hand grips the back of my neck, his fingers moving into my hair. Five minutes ago, I might have slapped it away, concerned he'd mess it up before people saw it. Now, I couldn't care less.

"Hey, Nik!" A sharp banging on the window startles us. "Come on, man, let's go."

Nik stares at me. "I might have to hit Kyle with a soccer ball, on purpose."

"Not funny." I tap his shoulder.

It kinda is funny now that I'm all healed, but I won't tell him that.

"You wait right there," he says before he helps me out of his truck.

After taking our picture in front of an arch of balloons and a backdrop with the school colors and Saint mascot, Nik leads me by the hand into the gym.

The homecoming committee decorated this place with streamers and balloons. Above the dance floor, there's a lighted net. It doesn't look like it's tall enough for many of the guys to fit under, but time will tell. The dimmed lights and strobing lights swirl from one wall, then the next. "Wanna dance?"

Every student is on the floor when "Perfect" by Ed Sheeran crackles to life. "This song is magnificent," I whisper, swaying to the soft beat.

"Compared to your magnificence, it's a mere speck of dust."

Nik's words are sweet summer berries—the ones we picked together in a local Sicilian vineyard. They seal my feelings for him, capturing my heart and making it his.

His familiar touch produces a wave of warmth, surging through me as his hands find their home on my waist, his smile radiating pure happiness. Mine wrap around his neck. My fingers trace the curve of his neck and then tangle in his hair just as I melt into him. A sigh of utter joy escapes my lips and the world around us fades away.

25

"If you're not comfortable out here, we can go back to the gym," he murmurs, as he rests his forearm on the wall next to my head.

No, thank you. I feel the tenderness of his words all the way to my toes. My teeth graze the side of my lip quickly. "I like being here with you," I say, forcing myself to meet his gaze.

After dancing for an hour like it was going to be outlawed, I asked Nik if we could get some air. He clearly misunderstood. With every movement, he brings himself closer to me and I lose even more air.

"So, you're okay if I kiss you?"

My pulse spikes. I've been imagining what it would be like to kiss Nik. Could we do that here in the school hallway? Not my first choice, but we are alone. My cheeks heat, and I press my cold fingers against my face, cooling them, giving me a chance to respond.

I nod, unwilling to spare the small amount of breath swirling around in my lungs. I am on reserve with Nik this close, intoxicating me with his crisp ocean air scent. When the corner of my mouth curls slightly and he grins at me, I shake my head, knowing something cocky is going to come out of his mouth.

"I'm gonna need a verbal confirmation to make sure this is okay," he says as the fingers of his free hand gingerly trace my collarbone, sending shivers down my spine that vibrate through my body, anticipating pure delight.

You've dreamt of this day for years. Be brave. Be bold. Kiss this guy!

"It's okay."

He leans closer, but doesn't kiss me on the lips as I expected. Wanted. Trailing kisses down my neck, stopping to nuzzle my neck, he asks. "Just okay?"

"I guess that depends on how good you are at this." The low chuckle in my ear is perfect. I definitely wasn't looking for a number of girls he'd kissed in our time away. That's a conversation for another time when I can think straight and my heart isn't threatening to jump out of my chest. *Or maybe never.*

"Orchids are my favorite," is all he says after he inhales, but before his eyes lock with mine. He looks just as nervous as I feel.

The warm, unspoken plea in his gaze leaves me aching for our first kiss.

I reach for the open flaps of his suit jacket and pull him flush with me.

"I guess I have my answer."

He tilts my head like he's a kissing pro. Not seventeen-year-old Nik Valentino from Catina, Sicily, who used to throw mud at me. His firm lips dance with mine as he slides his hands down and grabs my hips, pressing his large hands into my skin, pulling me impossibly closer to his chest.

I don't know how long this delicious kissing session lasts, but when Nik pulls back with a ragged breath, mirroring mine, and asks, "Are you still okay with this?" I blurt out my answer without thinking.

"Maybe."

"Maybe?"

Panic jolts my heart like an AED machine, but there's no turning back now.

"Keeley…" his voice trails off, waiting for me to answer.

It's now or never. I'll either get more electrifying kisses or this will be the shortest relationship in history.

"I'm okay with this if you are." *Okay, a bit of a cop out, but it's not a lie.* Like he asked me before, *What's wrong with wanting reassurance?*

His hands move to my arms. Even with that shift, my blood flows like hot lava through my veins. I inhale and exhale to regain some composure. There's no way I won't sound affected by this guy. My gaze drifts from his eyes to his mouth and back again. His mouth twitches, a prelude to his ever-present dazzling grin. Obviously, he's enjoying my nervousness a little too much.

"I'm wild about you. For the last two years I've been like a lost puppy without you. Now, I feel alive."

That deep, husky voice, that always makes my heart race, whispers its admission, leaving me breathless. I press my palm to my stomach to ease my tense muscles and settle the twister of emotions swirling about, as my gaze drops to the floor.

What if Nik and I end up getting married and he takes his dad's place? The notion of me as a mafia boss's wife is so ridiculous that I would laugh, if it weren't a possible reality.

Both his hands cup my face gently. "I know it's hard for you to trust people, so I don't expect you to just believe me. In time, I'll show you that you're safe with me."

"Thank you." I meet his gaze. It's silently telling me I have to make the next move. There is something attractive about a guy who won't push things to the next level. I know he'd go back to the dance or even take me home this second if I said so. To be clear: that's the last thing I want. My heart flips at how protected and cared for Nik has made me feel.

What if he's really good with words? Those Italian guys know how to sweep girls off their feet with their dreamy eyes and smooth words.

I realize my silence has made him nervous when he starts to say, "Keeley, why don't we—"

But I cut him off when I use his open suit jacket to press up slightly on my toes and run my hand through his hair, softly murmuring, "In the meantime, I don't think it would be too bad if we kissed."

He grins and that boyish smile I love so much fills his face as his arms find my waist and he tugs me even closer, removing all the space between us. "Anything for you." His lips are on mine in an instant. They feel so soft, yet firm. Nik's kisses are gentle and his hands traversing my back sent goosebumps...everywhere!

Unlike our first kiss moments ago, he flicks his tongue against my bottom lip, causing my insides to tremble.

As I open my mouth, Nik deepens the kiss. One of his hands grips the back of my neck, tilting it slightly. His fingers weave through my hair, sending tingles deep into my scalp.

The sound of music gets louder, like someone opened the gym door and Nik pulls back, his breathing labored like mine. Running his hand through his hair, he says, "We should get back in there before we get too carried away."

"Definitely." We haven't had <u>the</u> talk yet. With Nik saying he doesn't rely on God anymore, I wonder how he'll take the news that I plan on honoring God by not having sex until I'm married.

26

MOST COUPLES TEND TO get closer after they kiss. Keeley freezes in place. It's almost been a full week since homecoming and we're still just giving each other pecks on the cheek at school. Since her dad still didn't want me anywhere near her, I don't know when our next real date will be.

Maybe he'll change his mind once he closes the case on my dad. I learned Keeley's family lived in Italy to shut down the mafia's activity. My blood boils to know he's been involved in so many crimes, many of which I don't know the details of since they're classified.

It's also petrifying that my Uncle Sal and his goons, or maybe they're my dad's goons, have increased their phone calls. Mr. James has a mirror image of my phone, so he can keep one step ahead of whatever is expected to go down.

Unfortunately, that also means I can't text Keeley anymore, and she can't text me. Her dad told me to keep things about my family quiet, even from Keeley. That didn't stop me from telling her not to text me because her dad wouldn't like it. *So far, so good.*

Glancing over at her working with Grayson on her follow through, I imagine our next date. Without spoiling my plan, I can easily say it will include her three favorite things: activity, ice cream, and me.

No, I am not full of myself, just hopeful that I make the top three.

"Hey, Nik," Vinny slaps me on the shoulder, pulling me back to the soccer game that is a must win. We have had a lot of those lately. We already made it into the playoffs, but now we have to win or lose based on the seed we want.

"I'm really sorry for what I put Keeley and you through." I nod.

Vinny has apologized so many times it's borderline annoying. In fact, Keeley already told him to stop apologizing. I don't know how she does it, but she'd forgiven him without question. She said it was all God and had nothing to do with her.

"Coach convinced me I had to..." Vinny shifts his eyes to the ground.

I know that feeling. My dad could convince Mother Nature to make it snow in Florida.

"Look, Keeley's forgiven you. It's over now."

He bounced the ball on his knee. "I never realized the rough life you had."

Should I tell him that I had a great life up until my mom died? That was the night I found out about the family business—something I still want no part of.

"All that glitters isn't gold."

Vinny shakes his head. "No, man. Don't bring Shakespeare into this. I get enough of him in English class."

We laugh.

"What are you doing over here?"

"We're making peace," Vinny says.

Brent claps both our shoulders. "That's good to hear. It's game time. Have you seen them play?" He jerks his head toward the other side of the field. "All of you have to work like you're the best of friends in order to win."

"Sounds like a plan, Coach," Keeley says as she and Grayson join us.

The game is tied. It's been back and forth the entire time, but at least Mr. James cheers for her, instead of being on his phone. Kee's playing is next level for sure, but she can't do it alone.

With thirty seconds to go in the game, Beryl leaves her defensive position. Dribbling back up the field, Keeley is wide open, but Beryl dribbles more and loses the ball. The other team's defense boots the ball to their side of the field and without an extra person on defense, they score. We hang our heads in a devastating 4-3 loss.

"Don't worry, guys. We're still in the playoffs. It just means we have to play as a team to win the rest of our games this season to end up third seed."

Sure, Coach. Winning six straight games shouldn't be a problem, since we work so well together. My insides are smirking and giving him two thumbs up. *Knock it off. Brent is just trying to encourage us.* That's a lot better than tearing us down, like Coach Bucci did.

Speaking of, his wife called my grandparents and Keeley's parents, apologizing for her husband's actions. He reduced his sentence by turning on my dad. His family is being put in the Witness Protection Program.

"Are you okay?" I whisper to Keeley. She nods. "Can we talk after this?"

CONTENTMENT AND PLEASURE SAIL through me as I lean against Etna. Contentment because Keeley is smiling and holding my hand, and pleasure because this is Keeley—my girl.

"It's nice to see you happy. I'm surprised since we lost."

Her smile falters as if she just realized she should be sad. She holds onto a grin. "Coach Brent was explaining to Beryl the value of team-work. I think I heard him say she will be benched for the first half of the next game."

She's never one to relish in someone else's pain and it's not what I think she is doing now. She's happy that Beryl has consequences for her actions.

Don't worry, Keeley, I tell myself. I'll pay for my mistakes, too.

Fortunately, nothing in legal terms. Her dad took the boxes from under my bed and he made sure my grandparents' house had more cameras on the property than in a Hikvision factory. Power is scary.

Her dad and I didn't get any closer in terms of Keeley. He still wants me to stay away from her, but at least now I understand it's about my dad and not me.

Mr. James promised that he's monitoring my phone and he'll per-sonally watch the camera feeds he'd set up to his own cell phone.

"That's great, but I was hoping to talk about us,"

"Us? Is something wrong?" Keeley asks in a whisper.

I smooth out the lines forming between her eyebrows and then run my hand down my jaw. "I'm hoping you'll fill me in if there is." She scrunches her eyebrows even more.

My heart defeats my brain again when my hands reach for her, pulling her a little closer. "We haven't really kissed since homecoming. It's been a week." And I'm dying here. I don't tell her that, not wanting to scare her away.

Her hands whip to her face, hiding the beautiful pink hue I saw crawling up her neck at the mere mention of us kissing.

I peel her fingers away so I can see her sea-green eyes. They captivate me. "What's wrong?"

She quietly stares off into the wooded area. Meanwhile, my palms are sweaty despite the chilly October temperature. How could I have done something wrong already? Is she worried about my family's background? There's no sign that her dad gave her any details, but that doesn't mean he hasn't.

She sighs. "I'm a virgin and will remain one until I get married," she blurts out, still not able to look me in the eye. If I had to guess, she's staring at my nose. I hold back my laughter. The last thing I want is to make her feel as if I'm not in agreement with her decision—she is so darn cute, I can't help but smile or laugh when I'm around her.

But then her eyes slowly connect with mine while I let the silence sink in or give her another moment to say more if she wants.

"You told me I couldn't text you anymore, so I figured I was a bad kisser, or you wanted more and I wouldn't give it to you, so you wanted to let me down easily. I didn't want to make it any harder on you."

Harder on me? How did I get so lucky? My girl is perfect.

I pull her tight to my chest, wrapping my arms around her waist, like they haven't been aching to find their home again, like they had homecoming night. *Embrace the tingling sensation.* My heart kick starts into a pace that would impress Usain Bolt after an Olympic race.

My grin is unavoidable this time.

"Are you making fun of me?"

I shake my head. "No, ma'am. I'm wondering when you'll worry about yourself." My lips find her forehead and linger there, hoping to relax her tight muscles. "You shouldn't be worrying about making things harder on me. It's my job to protect you."

Mr. James was crystal clear about not telling Keeley anything about the Valentino Mafia family, but I can't have her thinking I'm rejecting her.

"I want you to text me, but..." But what? Aliens took my phone. I dropped it when I went zip lining with Brent the other day. It fell into the toilet. No, no, and no—thankfully.

Her brows raise, urging me to finish my thought. My stomach twists in knots. I won't lie to her. As a kid, my mom said one of the best pieces of advice from the Bible is something about the truth setting people free. She explained it to me in depth as a kid, but since then, it somehow lost the profound meaning it once had. I am, however, not so far gone that I don't get the basic principle. If I lie to Keeley, I will be a prisoner to even more lies. This will not bode well for me and my desire to build our relationship.

"You don't have to worry about me pushing you to do anything you don't want to. My mom would find a way to punish me from the grave if I didn't wait for marriage, too."

A gasp catches in her throat. Apparently stunned by my admission, she swallows hard and follows with a bright smile, one that makes the sun jealous and my heart leaps. *My girl is gorgeous.*

I take the smile as an invitation to kiss her. That and the fact she doesn't push me away as I tilt closer. She leans, too. I am so excited I could throw my fist in the air. Instead, I draw her to me, enjoying the softness of her body pressed against my chest as our lips meet in a tender kiss.

The nearly empty parking lot is not the place to get carried away, especially since want and desire are currently battling for control. I pull back, pressing a final, lingering kiss to her lips.

"Are you better?"

Her eyes flutter open. "Definitely."

Keeley's teeth tug at her lip. I promptly use my thumb to free it. "Don't be doing that, or we'll be here another hour. Your dad will send the National Guard after you."

"He's in the Navy, so he'd probably send SEAL Team Six." She laughs like it's actually funny that the toughest men in the world—the ones who captured Osama bin Laden—would be after me.

No, thank you. I kiss her on the check and open the door. I sneak one more kiss before I shut her door. Then, I hop in my truck. She won't leave until I'm ready. That's a big deal. Most girls drive away before her guy even gets to his truck.

I have to find a way to let Kee figure out my family dynamics on her own, unless I can convince her dad to share the news.

27

I WISH THIS OLDER version of Nik didn't have a cool edge to him. Then, maybe my chest wouldn't feel like it stepped directly into a sauna.

And don't forget about his personality. Whether he's demonstrating his confidence in soccer, his looks, or the fact that everyone likes him, he's doing so in a non-egotistical way. This makes him more appealing.

Have I mentioned his charismatic gentleman side? *Yum*! I can't get enough. Reaching for my hand, opening doors, wrapping me in warm hugs. Call me Olaf—I like warm hugs, as long as they come from Nik.

One playoff game dribbled into the next this past week, landing us the championship game. I'm feeding off the charged tension in the crowd.

"You ready, Sparky?" Nik asks, as he kicks a short pass my way.

"For sure. You?"

"Bet." We high five. Until my dad "allows" us to date, that's the only contact we can have.

When Trish trots out to center field with her team to practice their halftime routine (yes, she convinced her dad it would be a good idea to disrupt the soccer championship game with their dancing) she trails her fingers down Nik's arm and he shoos her away. When his eyes meet mine, the warmth radiating from them makes me feel wanted and cared for. Despite the frigid temperatures, my heart melts.

"You look like you're going to rip her hair out one strand at a time." Aurora passes me the ball.

It's amazing how some people can grow up and show kindness while others have to act like kindness is an eleventh plague. When I first arrived, Aurora didn't even acknowledge me. Now she's left Beryl's clutches and thinks for herself. *You go, girl!*

"Based on the snarl she just gave Nik and me, I think his rejection is embarrassing enough."

A soft chuckle escapes Aurora's lips. "You don't know how to be a mean girl, do you?"

"It's not something I ever aspire to be. Life is hard enough. Why put someone else down and make their journey any harder?"

"You're like a thirty-year-old living in a teenager's body."

I shrug. *Maybe.* The first Bible lesson my mom taught me was to treat others the way I want to be treated. "I'm not perfect...not even close, but I forgive people quickly. If they keep doing me wrong, I still forgive them, but eventually have to set boundaries, so my mental health isn't in jeopardy."

AFTER POWERING THROUGH THE first half of this game and ten minutes of the second, Coach pulls me to the bench. "Take a drink, Keeley, you're dragging out there. Are you okay?"

"There's only thirty minutes left. I can do better." He eyes me, probably letting me know I never answered his question.

He points toward the timekeeper. "Alright. Show me the Keeley I'm used to seeing."

Lord, I have to be imagining things. Help me to focus on the game. No one is in the woods. Everything is fine.

With my knee on the cold field, Nik steals the ball and I cheer. "Way to go Nik."

As if that encouragement was what he needed, Nik dribbles the ball up the field with a little give and go pass between him and Grayson—right between two opponents, epic! Nik scores, putting us ahead by one.

The referee calls me in while the other team sets up and I jump into Nik's arms. "I'm so proud of you."

They score quickly, tying the game again. In the final moments of the game, I steal the ball and dribble it the entire length of the field, with Nik running parallel. This can go either way. Both teams are playing excellent defense. Who's going to mess up? *Please not me, Lord.* A defensive player rushes me.

I pass ahead to Nik and cut to the inside, outrunning my opponent. Nik passes the ball a little higher than I anticipate and I have to sprint. The goalie is rushing to the ball. Who'll get there first? Me! With the goalie high, it only takes a swift kick to score a goal. We are back up by one. *This game has been a killer.*

The other team rushes to reset, hoping they can score fast and tie-up the game, pushing us into overtime. I don't blame them, I'd be the same way.

The tension is palpable; the weight of the championship rests on every play.

Our opponents kick the ball, and the clock doesn't start. Spectators and Coach Brent are yelling at the operator to start it, while the opponent's coach is grinning.

Fighting with the ref won't help, so I steal the ball and kick it out. Then the clock starts.

Whatever.

Now the coach for the other team is causing a fit…with the clock running. *Some people don't use their heads.*

I imagine she's frustrated. We're going to win this. I can feel it. I imagine all she can see is their championship opportunity slipping through their fingers. Devastating. That's not sarcasm, either. I would be heartbroken if the roles were reversed.

Joy bubbles in my chest when the buzzer sounds. We offer a round of *"good game"* and high-fives before heading to our bench.

Nik picks me up and spins me around. His muscles tense, and he slowly lowers me to the ground. Shock splays across his face.

"Are you okay?"

He's jittery. Not in an excited, *we just won the championship game* kind of jittery. *What* spooked him?

"Come on, Coach wants us." Nik looks over his shoulder as he guides me back to the bench.

Coach nailed it—my head wasn't in the game. The entire time, I felt like someone was watching me. Not spectators. I mean creepily. Was someone hiding in the woods? Of course not. It's possible I've listened to too many true crime podcasts.

My dad hasn't missed a game and though he's not overly praising me, he's not criticizing everything I do anymore. Mom told me that he's trying to make an effort.

He told EJ the same thing, but it doesn't feel like an effort when he allowed EJ to date Liz, but he's still mad that I didn't tell him myself about going to homecoming with Nik. *The man finds everything out!*

Brent's voice pulls me in. "This has been a tough season, but you learned to work as a team and won the Championship. I am so proud of all of you." Coach Brent puts his fist out and we all bump it.

The look on Nik's face isn't the joy of winning the biggest game of the season. No. It reminds me of little kids who think there's a boogeyman waiting to pop out of their closet.

"Look at these champs!" My dad's authoritative voice looms over the team. "Coach, can I see Nikolaus, please?"

Brent lifts his pointer finger and nods. "Let's pray."

When Coach finishes, Nik barely grazes my pinky and whispers, "I'll be back."

With an arm around Nik's shoulders my dad leads him in the opposite direction, nearly whispering in his ear. *Now I know something is fishy.*

A shiver courses down my spine as I swear I see movement in the woods. No. It's getting dark. I have to be mistaken. My chest isn't even tight—my first indicator of danger, or perceived danger—and my breathing is controlled.

Why would my dad and Nik keep things from me? I really hope I didn't set myself up to be let down again. My father is known for this vicious cycle—having the people around him let their guard down, then using everything they've said or done against them. Sometimes he'll do things and then hold it over the person's head like reverse blackmail or something.

And what's the deal with Nik? I can't text him. That seems like a red flag from the Cheaters 101 handbook (I think I just made that up, but it works).

Now a knot of anxiety tightens in my chest and the lingering scent of regret hangs in the air as I wonder if I'd made a mistake, letting them both back into my life.

28

NIK

MORNING MINGLES WITH THE mess from yesterday. The only reason I peel my eyelids open is because Keeley is coming over.

Yesterday, I pushed myself to impress her during the grueling game. Her reward hugs lit my skin on fire. Today, I'm dragging.

Honestly, everything until I caught a glimpse of Uncle Sal in the parking lot with his goons, was dope. But Mr. James is all over the situation.

Questions that aren't important run through my head. *Does he have a passport? How long is he here for? Does my dad know he's here? Did my dad send him?*

Okay, I know the last two questions might be really important—in fact, the potential answer to the last one sends shivers down my spine—but the others are mere distractions.

If my dad sent him, what does that mean? Is he going to kill me since I won't take his place in the family business? A father wouldn't kill his son for that, would he?

It's been over a year. Someone must have replaced me by now. I suppose it's possible that my dad is that powerful to be still running things from prison. Why me, then?

My heart races with equal parts fear and adrenaline. Fear of the answers, and thrilled for my time with Keeley.

I grab my phone from the nightstand—11AM. Her dad is dropping her off at noon.

Yeah, he's not on board with us being anything other than teammates or peers. Since we have to finish our assignment, he agreed to let her come over. He's a scary dude and might kill me if he knew how many times a day I thought about kissing his daughter.

But he's also the one keeping my grandparents and me safe from my dad and uncle. So there's that.

It's not lost on me he wouldn't let Keeley drive over herself. EJ has to work the closing shift and they don't want to pick him up. Kee could have picked up EJ, but it's obvious Mr. James wants to monitor her, or me, or both of us.

How do I plan to explain to Keeley that we can't sneak kisses or hug when my grandparents aren't hovering like a Sikorsky UF-60 Black Hawk? No clue. Suggestions welcomed. Email them to *you'reintroub le@NikmightloseKeeleyagain.com*

Maybe the dramatic girls at schools are rubbing off on me. Yuck.

For real, I think I'll write her a note and leave it for her to see. *Sorry, Keeley, we can't kiss or hug today because your dad is watching this house and listening to everything going on through cameras he set up because my family threatened you and they want me to be a mafia boss.*

Nope! That's not the answer. A perfect idea pops into my head. I'll have my grandpa let her in and say we have to work at the table today.

Wuss. Cop out. My heart and brain finally agree on something. Unfortunately, it's about how much of a coward I am being about this. On the one hand, I want to tell Keeley everything. But her dad gave me specific instructions not to.

Would it be such a horrible thing to win over her dad by following his order? Yes, if Keeley pulls away from me. Admittedly, I'm carrying out his wishes because I'm worried about her safety.

A knock at my door pulls me from my awful cover up ideas. "Come in."

"You're not up yet?" my grandpa barks. "Your girl will be here in less than an hour," he says, checking his watch. "You need to clean up—yourself and this room."

Great, now my grandpa thinks I need hygiene reminders, like I'm in elementary school. *You're acting like you are.*

Isn't it annoying when people seem to have things all figured out and instead of helping, they sit back and watch you struggle? Welcome to my life, where civil war wages within me constantly.

"I figured we'd work at the table today."

Grandpa shrugs. "Okay. Your grandmother and I are going to the church to help plan for the Operation Christmas Child packing party next week. If you're not doing anything then, maybe you and Keeley could join us and pack a box or two."

So, there goes my plan. Man up... *Figure it out.*

The OCC packing party sounds like something Keeley would like. Maybe we should go.

"Mom's disappointed in me, isn't she?"

Grandpa moves closer. "May I?" he asks, pointing to the edge of my bed.

"She's probably sad that your dad put you in this situation, but how could anyone feel let down by you?"

I shrug, thinking of many reasons.

"You didn't follow in your dad's footsteps. That alone is reason enough to be proud of you."

"What are we going to do?"

Grandpa doesn't waver. "Whatever Mr. James says. I wish he'd thought to use you or Rachel in Italy. She might still be alive."

I open my mouth to speak, but he continues. "I don't blame him. Honestly, I blame your mom a little, your grandmother, and myself."

"Why?" I've never asked for answers. I guess I didn't want to know if my mom or grandparents knew about my dad's occupation.

He stares over my shoulder, studying the wall behind me as if transporting himself to another time. "Rachel said she'd protect you, wouldn't let you become what your dad is slash was."

"She knew?" Shock sunbursts through my chest.

He nods.

"I was fifteen when Keeley left. Why didn't she tell me then? Why didn't she tell Keeley's mom? We knew Mr. James was a high-ranking official."

"We were all scared. If we said something and the American government couldn't or wouldn't help, he would have killed both of you then." He rubs the stray tears from his cheek.

"How'd you not turn your back on God?" I cringe. Saying this out loud proves I did.

"He doesn't promise a life of roses and honey. Paul tells us we will have trials."

Grandpa leans forward, reaching under my night stand and pulling out my dusty Bible—the one Mom gave me after I got baptized in the Mediterranean, with Keeley.

"This is a hard trial. Waking up daughterless every day isn't the way it's supposed to be. In humans' minds, parents die first, but God is the boss."

He flips to the New Testament. "At least I didn't have to see it." Scanning the page for a particular verse, he finds it and begins reading. "Near the cross of Jesus stood his mother..."

Grandpa weeps as he reads. As a faithful man, his tears probably have more to do with Jesus's death as much as my mom's.

"He said to his mother, 'Dear woman, here is your son,' and to the disciple, 'Here is your mother.'"

He shuts the book, but leaves his head bowed. "If I had to watch Rachel die and have another daughter appointed to me..." He shakes his head.

Jesus is someone special. *Duh!*

His tears are flowing like Niagara Falls, taking me back to the day of her funeral. He had my mom's body transported to the states, so we could have her close.

Grandpa uses his hand to wipe his face. "That's enough of that."

He stands, moving toward the door. Then reminds me, "Don't do anything I wouldn't, especially since Mr. James watches the camera feed like lives depend on it."

They do, but he doesn't need that reminder.

"I love you, Son, so does your grandmother and your mom. But no one loves you as much as God does. He's waiting for you. Let him in, again."

I throw off my covers and wrap my grandpa in a hug. You know, one of those hugs that would make Grandma sigh, "Awww," if she saw it.

One thing I've learned is not to let moments slip away. We are not guaranteed tomorrow, so no one ever knows the last time they'll see a loved one.

It's not clear who releases first, but Grandpa has one departing sentence. "I am proud of you for standing up to your dad. Don't let these goons convince you to change. God is with you whether you acknowledge Him or not, so you might as well. He's the best to have on your side since He knows what's coming."

The soft click of my door does nothing to make me move. I stare at it like it has answers. Spoiler alert—it doesn't.

An alert on my phone rocks me from my thoughts. Keeley will be here in twenty minutes. I scramble to find clothes, tossing them on the bed.

Unexpectedly, I freeze staring at the Bible half covered by my jeans. I'm like a slo-mo video walking toward the bed, reaching for God's Word and plopping down.

"Show me where you want me, Lord." I haven't said that in years. The moment I do, an instant lightness fills me and freedom washes over me.

For the next fifteen minutes, I read. The Gospel of John sucked me in like it used to when Keeley and I read the Bible together.

Ding, Dong.

I jump. Five minutes to twelve; she's early. I find a piece of paper and shove it in the Gospel.

So much for a shower. I scurry to throw on my jeans and a sweat-shirt. My fingers glide through my hair several times. God knows what He is doing—who needs a comb anyway? Not me.

I do, however, need a toothbrush. Unwilling to keep Keeley wait-ing, I grab it and a tube of toothpaste. I shove them into the front of my hoodie and run down the stairs to get the door. I'll brush them after I let her in.

Colossal mistake.

If Keeley is my ray of sunshine, Uncle Sal is the torrential downpour combined with Category 5 hurricane winds.

This can't be happening.

"Hey, nephew." He steps forward, slapping my cheek once—hard-er than necessary—making me want to pulverize him. "You didn't think you could run from us forever, did you?"

His two goons walk in, bumping me with their shoulders, making their intentions known. The tall, bulky one who reminds me of Tony Soprano is grinning at me like the Grinch, and I imagine he's think-ing... *You're all mine. I'll do what I'm told, but when it's time to eliminate you, I'll be happy to send you down the river.*

The second one is none other than Coach Bucci. "How'd you get out of jail? Have you been working for him or my dad all this time?" He remains silent.

Dread shoots down my spine as I look out the door before shutting the wooden rectangle, trapping me inside with these monsters.

"You didn't think your dad and I would leave you unattended to forget about us, did you?"

This can't be happening. I search out the window for Keeley.

"Don't worry, your girl will be a little late."

I recoil. Their sinister laughing grates on my nerves and I lunge toward Sal, but the Soprano wannabe blocks me.

"If you hurt her or her family—"

"You'll what?" Sal mocks. "You're powerless since you let your family down."

I'm grateful for all the cameras in here. I know Mr. James must be seeing this and he'll be here soon. As long as Sal and his goons didn't hurt him.

Please, God, no.

Lord, I know I just got back in your good graces less than thirty minutes ago, but please guide me. What should I say? Do? Not say or do? Let Mr. James see and hear what he needs to put these criminals away. Keep Keeley and her family safe. Watch out for Grandma and Grandpa. In Jesus' name, Amen.

Behind me, the distinct sound of a gun slide pushing a bullet into the chamber causes me to freeze.

This is so much worse than yesterday.

Okay, Boss, you're in charge. Please forgive me for any sins I've committed and omitted. You are my savior.

I let out a deep sigh. "I'm ready."

29

"COME ON, EJ, WE'RE late." I am supposed to be at Nik's in five minutes and it takes ten to get there.

Dad and I are in the garage trying to figure out what is wrong with Etna. She's been spitting and sputtering since I drove home from the game last night.

I still can't believe we're champions.

"It's not my fault you're in a rush to see your boyfriend."

The sound of a metal tool clinking against the cement floor alerts EJ that we aren't alone. I'm frozen. EJ's wide eyes and incomprehensible arm movements are telling me something. What? I don't know.

By the grace of God, my wits return. "Why don't you tease someone else, like your actual girlfriend, since I don't have a boyfriend?"

Yeah, that should do it, right?

My dad's eyes, burning a hole through me, say *wrong*.

Please, Lord. Help. Any other words would be futile. He knows what dad needs to calm down. Me? I'm clueless and scared silly.

"I told you to stay away from that boy."

Dad's phone, perched on his hip, is beeping, but he silences it. I gasp. Dad has never done that ... ever.

"Actually, you told me to spend some time with him. Remember about a week after we arrived, you made me go to the youth group, mentioning Nik specifically by name to hang out with?"

Dad stares at me with the calmness I've only seen when he's working.

The phone beeps again, getting the same treatment.

I hope no one is in trouble. My dad has a high-profile position, keeping people safe. This isn't fair to them if they are counting him.

The fierce growl emitting from my dad's throat is one that a grizzly bear would cower to. All the calmness exuded from minutes ago, is a distant memory. EJ, the one who started this, headed back inside. *Thanks, jerk.*

Apparently, you need me in Heaven, Lord. I'll be there soon, I think as my dad inches closer to me. Tears are already spilling down my cheeks. I've never seen him this angry. No doubt, I won't be able to see Nik through a plate-glass window at this point. It's possible both fear and sadness stain my cheeks.

Normally, I can keep them at bay because my anger takes over. Not this time.

More beeping from the phone. Silenced again. *Sorry, Buddy, I know how you feel.* I wonder if other people talk to objects when they're petrified?

"I told you, 'Don't get mixed up with that boy', didn't I?"

EJ returns with Mom. Okay, so he's not the jerk I thought he was—I should have known.

"Settle down honey," Mom tries to calm the red-faced man glaring at me.

"The lengths I went to keep you two apart. That's all ruined. He's from a dangerous family. You don't have a clue what the world is like, yet you want to act like an adult."

I'm seventeen freaking years old. Okay, now the anger is rushing in like a scorching desert, sopping up any remaining tear drops.

"Have you learned more? Is Nik in danger, too?" Mom is the first to question my dad.

But I don't give him a chance to answer because something else he said finally registers in my brain. "What did you do to keep us apart besides taking my Vespa that day?"

See, I knew my dad was responsible for my unhappiness. He claims he does things because he loves me. Nope.

More beeping. Silenced again. *That's so ignorant.*

Lord, please protect whoever is trying to get in touch with my dad. You are more powerful anyway.

"I might as well tell all of you. Nik's dad is in prison. He's a powerful mafia boss. We were in Italy specifically to get enough dirt on Mr. Valentino to shut down his operation. Unfortunately, the department I work for couldn't waste any more resources after being in Italy for two years and not getting any closer, so they sent me to Ohio to track down a person in witness protection who was there because of his or her involvement with the Valentino family business."

My gut twists and I throw up on my dad's spot-less garage floor. Don't think for a second I won't hear about that.

"We're monitoring his uncle. He's in America, most likely trying to take Nik back to Italy."

This day is getting better and better.

I gasp. "You used me!" I burst out. "How dare you? You couldn't do your own job, so you had me become friends with him and learn what I could. You rat."

"Don't you call me names, little girl. We need to keep bad guys off the street and keep families safe."

"Except your own."

"Watch your tongue," Dad barks, pointing his finger at me.

The sympathy radiating off EJ and Mom's face are too much for me to handle and I throw up again.

"You used Mom, too," EJ barks. "Keeley's been right about you all along. What is your problem with her?"

I wipe my mouth. EJ finally sees it. One look at my mom, and I knew she does, too. "That's why you kept encouraging me to hang out with Rachel and got mad when I wanted to work. You fought with me for ten months while I got my cosmetology degree and that's because I couldn't do your work."

You tell him, Mom.

I check my watch. It's now five past noon. I was supposed to be at Nik five minutes ago.

Dad's phone rings this time. He silences that, too. *Enough!*

"Someone is obviously in trouble. You can't just ignore people, letting them down. You have a job to do."

He ignores me like I'm some kid who doesn't know what I'm talking about.

Whatever. You'll pay the consequences.

"I'm turning eighteen in a few months, then there's nothing you can do to stop me from seeing Nik." *Isn't that what I really want?* That's a question I'll have to deal with later. I can only handle one big issue at a time.

He crosses his arms over his chest. "You are not to see that boy. He's bad news."

"You don't even know him. You're judging him based on his father's actions, like you judge other people."

"Apples don't fall far from the tree."

"Thankfully, I fell from mom's side of the tree." I bet we'd laugh about that comment if the room wasn't buzzing with tension.

A force stronger than mine says the next words. "Since you have no respect for me, I have none for you." *That's not what the Bible says*, my mind scolds, unable to stop the freight train of thoughts.

I'm in Etna before I know it, with my foot on the brake, praying the car starts up…no more spitting and sputtering. *Help me get out of here.*

After two attempts, she sputters to life. *I'll take it. Thank you, Lord.*

My mom is at my window. "Baby, you are too upset to drive. Please don't leave like this. I'll drive you wherever you want."

Through the closed passenger window, I hear EJ trying to convince my dad to say something to make me stay.

Instead, when I glimpse at EJ, I see Dad…on his phone.

"Keeley. Nik is in trouble. I'm heading there now," Dad yells as he runs to his truck.

I see my mom crying. I should stay, but I have to prove my point. Captain James will not be my boss forever. "I love you, Mom, but I have to see Nik. Dad is probably just making that up because he knows I'm a chicken."

"I love you," Mom croons.

I blow her a kiss and Etna is out of the garage before she can stop me. I feel awful. I love my mom, but she's the one who tells me I won't have her forever. I have to find my way in the world. If Nik will be involved with the mafia in the future I need to know.

When I look in my rearview mirror, I see EJ holding my mom.

Thanks bro, I own you one.

30

"THIS ISN'T NECESSARY," I growl, refusing to show pain as one of Uncle Sal's goons link my hands through the back of the chair and zip ties my wrists.

Sal crouches beside me. "But it is. I can't have you lunging at me again."

His pungent breath, a mix of coffee, eggs, and who knows what else, churns in my gut.

Mine's not that bad. I think of my toothbrush and paste stored in my sweatshirt.

"I can see you have my big brother's temper, so I won't take my chances." He slaps my cheek and stands to his full height. Comically, it's three or four inches below his shortest goon.

My uncle checks his watch again. His pacing is making me anxious. Where is Keeley's dad? Hopefully, his phone alerted him and left Keeley at home. I'd never forgive myself if something happened to her.

"Things will go real smooth if you give me the packages delivered here."

"I refused all deliveries. Didn't my dad tell you?" Mr. James took the package my grandmother signed for, but I don't know its contents.

"Your dad isn't running the show anymore, I am!" His sinister smile flashes in front of me and that torrid breath sends a wave of nausea through my gut.

"Okay."

He growls at my one-word answer.

He pulls a gun from his waistband and presses the cool steel against my forehead. Despite his shaky voice, Sal's hand is surprisingly still.

"Think you're funny?" I shake my head, fully alert. "This isn't how it was supposed to end; with me killing my own nephew." A nervous tremor runs through me as I swallow hard, the lump of fear refusing to budge.

I stare at him with what I hope is sympathy and not challenging him to shoot me. "Please tell me what you did to make Keeley late?"

The cruel rasp of his laughter echoes through the room, raising goosebumps on my skin.

So help me if he...

As my body tensed, Sal relaxed. The bit of air between my skin and the gun's barrel feels freeing, like a gale force wind.

"Some minor car trouble." Sal smiles, proud of his actions.

Lord, please be with Keeley. I don't know what this monster did, but I trust in God to set things right.

"You know you don't have to do this, right?" I brave the question and he jams the gun back into my forehead.

I'll have a circle indented there for sure. One might expect me to be more terrified with a gun pointed at my head.

Don't think for a second I'm not.

My heart is pounding like a war drum, my hands are clammy. I half wonder if I can just slip out of the zip ties. Impending death looms over this room. A place my grandmother has pictures of my mom strategically placed to make her feel better. *I'm not sure that it always does.*

If I act any different from my normal joking self, Sal will become even more skittish, and then... I hate to think what he'll do to me. Or worse—Keeley. The stakes were too high now for me to change.

"Stop! This ends now. Give me the package." His raging outburst causes his whole body to shake, while disgust fills his features.

Clearly, I misread something...

"I don't have your packages. Can't you just get more of whatever it was?"

"Can't I just get more?" Sal waves the gun as he mocks my question. "NO!"

Sal grabs a chair identical to mine and slams it against the floor, breaking the back off when he throws it against the floor. He slams the remaining seat to the floor, forcing me to slide my feet back toward my body.

"Let me educate you. In our family, the eldest son takes over the business. It's been that way for nearly two hundred years. If that son dies before he has a son, the next oldest brother would take over..."

Light bulbs flash in my mind, and I nod.

He slaps my face with two quick successions.

Don't react. He's not worth losing my cool or Keeley. Understatement of the century. I look out the window after hearing what I think is the soft click of a door. The goons don't budge and my uncle is apparently having too much fun slapping me to focus on anything else.

Please send help.

"With you gone, I can go back home and take over the business and..."

Sal gets a text and doesn't finish his sentence, but I get the drift.

Fight. I hear my mom's voice. Sal wants the package, but he wants me dead to take over. If he thinks I know where the package is, he won't kill me until he gets it.

"Prove to me Keeley is alive, and I'll take you to the package," I say, all the while shifting my wrists, hoping to loosen them. I freeze when I feel a trickle of liquid down my palm. Blood.

Lord, please show me the way out of this.

His sinister cackle and the cool metal now pressed to my cheek make me nervous, while his vomit-worthy breath makes me sick. "You naïve excuse for a human. I don't need you." He emphasized the word need. "I'm already getting what I want."

He turns his phone toward me. I lose it when I see Etna smashed to smithereens.

"You monster." I'm on my feet in his face. All the dirt bag does is laugh at me.

"If you would have convinced her to take the drugs from this guy, she would have died after one dose. We made them special for her. At least her car didn't blow up like your mother's."

Realization hits me and I knee him hard in the groan. His upper body careens toward the floor, but I catch him and knee him again. This time, blood splatters from his nose instantly as he flops to the floor, rocking in the fetal position.

"You killed my mother, you piece of crap?" A rhetorical question, but he still answers with a bitter laugh, like he's proud.

His goons force me to sit again. The tall one shadows Bucci, who currently has his gun pointed at me.

I'll have to process later. *Lord, please don't let Keeley die.*

"Give me the package now," Sal grits through his teeth as he returns to a nearly standing position.

I open my mouth to tell him for the millionth time that I don't have his package when a voice behind me brings a wave of relief to my soul.

"Come and get your package. I have it." Keeley's dad is every bit as scary as I've always believed. "But first, you let the boy go."

"They hurt Keeley. She was in an accident," Nik declares.

With the speed of light, Mr. James pulls his handgun from his hip and shoots Bucci—the only one holding a gun. The Tony Soprano look-alike draws his gun, but not quick enough. They lay motionless on the floor.

With the gun now pointed at Sal, he instructs the man to cut me free with a pair of scissors Mr. James extracted from his vest.

"Tell me where that accident was."

When Sal doesn't say anything, Keeley's dad shoots him in the foot. "We do anything for family, right?"

Sal shakes his head with such force that I am afraid his neck will snap, but we get the information we need.

Mr. James speaks with authorities, sending his daughter the help she needs and instructs me to leave.

"The boy is coming out."

The half dozen military men stationed on my front lawn alarm me. Thank goodness, he announced my exit.

Stepping outside, the sun is fighting to push beyond the clouds. *That's right. Keep fighting. Thank you, Lord, for saving me. Now please help Mr. James and Keeley.*

31

NIK

"HI. WHERE CAN I find Keeley James?" The receptionist, perched under the welcome sign at Cumberland Regional Hospital, looks at me like I have eight heads.

"Um. Car accident victim; brought in about two hours ago," I add, figuring the missing info will help get the answers I need.

"May I see identification, please?"

Absolutely. I didn't think it would be this easy.

Her eyes scan my license. With a flicker of pity across her face, she returns it. "I'm sorry, Mr. Valentino, but family only."

Drat. I sigh and force a smile.

Unwilling to leave, I sit. My phone in my hands, crafting a text for EJ.

Before I send it, Mr. James barrels through the door carrying a metal lock box and I'm on my feet.

"Are you okay?" I ask, seeing the slashes on his face.

He nods. "Where's Keeley?"

"They won't let me see her. Family only."

Mr. James draws in a breath, pulling out his phone, studying it. He quickly reads a text I assume is from Mrs. James. "Keeley is out of recovery and doing fine. She'll have a room shortly."

We both sigh with relief and plop into chairs beside one another. He rests the metal box on his lap and bows his head over it.

The weathered profile of Keeley's dad looks at least ten years older than he did when he walked into my house earlier. I'm nervous about asking how things played out for his men.

"Are you sure you don't need medical attention?" Nik asks.

"Nik, I'm sorry, but your uncle didn't make it. I'll spare you the details, but know that he fought hard. We had no choice. Authorities transferred your dad to the Supermax section of L'Aquila District Prison until further notice."

I gasp. Everyone knows Supermax prisons mean solitary confinement.

"Your grandparents are safe at home. Tonight, my men and women returned to their families." He pauses, rubbing the back of his neck. "There's one more thing I need to address."

Mr. James pulls the box higher on his thighs, resting his elbows on his knees. He swipes his hand down his face twice.

Tension, thick as lard, sinks between us, and my gut wrenches. *What isn't he telling me?*

I jerk back when he rips himself from the seat and orders me to follow him.

"Where are we going?"

"To get my freedom back."

32

Keeley

"Do you need anything, honey? EJ can go get it." Mom asks.

"Thanks for volun-*telling* me."

Mom rests her palm on EJ's shoulders. "Sorry. I don't want to leave Keeley." He nods and smiles to show he's not upset about having to help.

"I'm fine." EJ pats her hand.

The door flies open and our heads whip in that direction.

"Dad. Nik? What's wrong?"

"I have to tell you something."

It's always about him. "I'm fine. Thanks for asking."

He hands his head and sighs. "I'm sorry. You're right." He reaches out his hand and places it on top of mine. "How are you feeling?"

"Like my spleen ruptured." No one laughs.

"Too early for spleen jokes?" I shrug.

"This is all my fault. I'm so sorry, Keeley." Nik rushes to the end of my bed and places his hand on my covered foot.

"How's this your fault? Police are looking for the guy who hit me."

"They found him," my dad interjects.

Mom claps. "Thank God."

Dad's expression is one of despair, something I haven't seen on his face … ever.

He hands Nik a metal box. His eyes pool with regret. "I'm sorry to both of you." He looks to me next. "These are yours."

"What are they?" I ask.

Nik holds up a finger, signaling me to wait.

"If I could explain myself, I would," my dad says, hanging his head.

The remorse on my dad's face differs from what I've seen in the past. Is he truly sorry? This must be big. What could he have done to be so apologetic?

"My mind had one mission, to catch Antonio Valentino in one of his acts. I clumped you together with your father, Nik, and I'm sorry. I was wrong."

"Wait!" I holler. "Someone give me my phone. Say that again, so I can have it on record that my dad made a mistake."

"Funny," Dad says with a short laugh.

Everyone laughs then.

"I see how happy Nik makes you. It'll be easier to make sure everyone is safe if he's close to our family."

"Rachel would appreciate you watching out for her boy," Mom says with a pool of tears threatening to slip down her cheek.

Nik holds out his hand to my dad. "We're good, right?"

"I'd hope so." He winks and changes positions, so that Nik is near my head.

Am I imagining this? "What's going on with you two and what's in the box?" I don't hesitate to ask.

"We'll open it together tomorrow. Since your mom's staying, I have to get back and check on my grandparents," Nik assures me.

"Not that we'd let you stay here anyway," EJ's stern brother voice makes him sound more like a parent.

Nik waves off the insinuation. "That's not what I meant."

EJ laughs. "I know. But it's funny to watch your reactions."

"Pay back with your girlfriend looms, so beware," I warn.

EJ shakes his head and I frown. He'll have to tell me what happened with Liz.

"I'll take the box with me. No peeking; I swear." He holds three fingers up like he was a boy scout in his younger years. "Tomorrow, I'm bringing another little surprise for you."

I beam at the thought of a surprise and melt when his cool lips kiss my warm forehead. "See you then!"

33

THE NEXT MORNING, I stare through the little window on the hospital door leading to Keeley's room. The doctor said she might be able to go home this evening if she doesn't have any complications from the laparoscopic surgery they performed to repair Keeley's spleen.

The nurse welcomed my plan when I explained it to her. She said that Keeley is the sweetest patient she's had so far this shift, but she has too much energy for a girl recently out of surgery.

I need to be brave—*no cop outs*. She needs to know how serious I am.

Only a solid, stainless steel door, smelling strongly of bleach and lemon, stands between Keeley and me. A mix of frustration and excitement battle within.

Frustration because this door is a symbol of the barriers that lay between us. I am still digesting the new information myself. This box Mr. James gave me feels like a ticking time bomb. No, a grenade. As soon as I open it, Keeley and I will either crash and burn together or we'll soar. Tough to say until she processes the information.

Regret fills me. Mr. James asked if I wanted him to tell Keeley everything, but I told him I would, saving him from his daughter's wrath.

He is a good man. He cares about his family, showing it the only way he knows how.

What's the problem?

Fear.

It pelts me with meteorite size debris. The anticipation of losing her again races through my veins like a waterslide.

She could tell me to buzz off. Kee might say she doesn't want to risk being closer to me because of my family history. Her dad has every available person checking into the mafia connections within my family. With Uncle Sal gone and Dad in solitary confinement with a future release date that will match the date on his death certificate, I hope there aren't any loose ties binding me to that life. I'd like to return to Sicily someday and I know Kee would like that, too. But she won't even consider it if danger lurks there.

Am I strong enough to be okay with her rejection, if that's what she gives?

I don't think so.

With strength not of my own, I push the door open and meet Keeley's eyes. Right away, I notice her finger wrapping around her hair.

Her mom is asleep on a cot the nurse must have brought in for her.

"Nik." I shift my focus back to Keeley. She gets more beautiful every time I see her. Even in a hospital gown, she lights up the room. There's only one word to describe her.

Breathtaking.

The air crackles with anticipation as Keeley's eyes sparkle, silently pleading for me to speak.

"Good morning, Nikolaus. How are you?" Mrs. James presses the tips of her fingers into her eyes and rubs circles before stretching both arms over her head as she stands tall.

"Hi." Great. I spoke a word, but did I have to wave awkwardly, too?

"Since you're here, do you think I could run to the cafeteria and grab some food while you stay with Keeley? I'm sure you have a lot to talk about." She winks at her daughter.

"Mom!" Keeley snaps. It's good to see surgery hasn't taken away her fire.

I laugh because it's obvious they were talking about me. That already feels like a win. "I'd love to watch over my girl." Kee smiles, turning her cheeks pink.

Once her mom leaves, I ask, "May I sit?" I point toward the bed. Her welcoming smile is all I see. "How are you feeling today?"

"Better now."

"Was something wrong before I got here?"

"Yes. No." She dips her chin, grumbles, and frowns.

Even though I have something special planned, I'll do anything to remove the sadness I see in her eyes.

"Trish showed up."

I rest my hand on her hip. "I'm so sorry I wasn't here."

She waves me off. "She came to apologize."

A sudden urge of shock rushed through me. "For real?"

"Kinda. She apologized for not getting to know me and for her part at the party." Keeley shrugs. "Trish is the "she" that the guy was referring to and the "he" was Coach Bucci." She shakes her head.

"Anyway, I guess her apology is something, but I think she'll still try to take you away from me."

"Never gonna happen. I promise."

"You can't promise me that."

I lean forward and kiss her forehead. "As long as you want me, I'll always be yours. Matching tattoos might drive home our commitment to one another."

She cringes. "Needles and I…"

Laughter bursts from my lungs. I remember her squeamish behavior around needles when I needed a tetanus shot.

"Don't laugh. You could get stuck with me."

"I'd never be *stuck* with you. I *choose* you. Every. Single. Time." Her breath hitches as I move closer. I drop a soft, lingering kiss on her cheek.

This must be a sign; my gut tells me to proceed with my plan. One of the two things will happen. It's possible God is a comedian and gives me the strength to push through my fear and Keeley will reject me, anyway. I am hopeful that does not happen, but there is always a possibility. The outcome I'm hoping for is obvious. She'll embrace my plan and all will be right with the world.

"Come on, beautiful, I'm breaking you out."

34

A FEW STRAGGLING BIRDS braving out the nearing winter temperatures sing in the distance. I'm grateful Nik brought me a coat. Though I wouldn't have minded wearing one of his sweatshirts instead.

Dad stayed last night until they kicked him out. He promised to be more accepting and understanding, learning about me and not passing any judgments or criticizing me constantly.

"Where are you taking me? Is it safe?"

"Do you think your mom or dad would let me take you anywhere unless they knew about it?"

Valid point, but that doesn't answer my question. Something is sus.

"Can you at least tell me the other surprise?" I clutch at the metal box Nik placed in my lap, anticipation surging through me like a live wire. I can't even guess what's inside. My heart thumps against my ribs. In a few minutes, everything could change.

He chuckles, reaching for the box.

"Hey, aren't we opening that?"

"*Prestu.*"

I tsk. "Soon. Really? Whatever's in there must be something big, or you wouldn't still be keeping it a secret."

He shakes his head and removes the box from my lap.

"Thank you for wheeling me out here. This is probably a beautiful garden in the spring and summer."

Nik nods, but remains silent. Then he takes a deep breath. I am starting to worry. What if he's moving back to Italy now that the threat seems over?

"Just tell me." I pull my jacket tighter, the cold air winding its way around my middle.

"Your dad kept our letters all these years. Except for one. I received it the day my mom died and authorities arrested my dad."

His words punch me in the gut, depleting my lungs of their oxygen. I didn't expect that. He opens the metal lid. Letters blossom over the brim, a delicate and beautiful sight.

"You wrote me." I release a soft breath.

When he nods, my heart soars, a triumphant burst of sunshine filling my chest and the morning sky!

He kisses the top of my head and wipes a warm tear shooting down my cheek.

"Don't be mad at him. He apologized. If you can forgive Vinny, you should be able to forgive your dad."

I know Nik is right. That doesn't stop the anger from boiling deep within. It's easy to forgive non-family members. When someone within your family betrays you, it cuts even deeper.

"He loves you and was trying to protect you from my dad. For that I'll always be thankful to him."

When it's put that way, Nik has a point. My anger will not disappear overnight, but I won't yell at my dad the next time I see him either.

Five minutes could have passed or five hours. Nik let me read one of his letters. It revealed how much he liked me and thought I was pretty. He's the only guy who's ever said I was beautiful and meant it. I'm not "one of the guys" to him.

I set the love letter back in the box and Nik's shaking fingers pull my attention.

"Nik, what are you doing?"

His knee must be freezing. Who kneels on the frozen earth?

The grin on his face mixes with nerves.

"Don't run. It's not what you think."

Me, run?

"Funny." I can't walk on my own, let alone run.

He inhales a deep breath and lets it out. It's visible in the frigid air. His eyes pin on me, telling me how much he cares.

"Keeley Madison James, once we're ready to get married and have a family and I ask you to be my wife, it'll be more grand than this ... and much, much warmer."

My hands fly to my mouth, covering it as I choke on the gulp of air I inhaled.

He slowly pulls off my glove, one finger at a time. It's as if he has all the time in the world, and it's not a bone-chilling twenty-degrees out. I push those thoughts out of my head and replace them with different ones. *This is super romantic and sweet.*

My legs are tingling, and it's not from the cold or the surgery. His slow, deliberate movements feel like an eternity. My heart pounds in my ears, rendering me useless.

He pulls out a little box from his jacket pocket.

"You said this isn't what I'm thinking ... you need to stick to your day job because you cannot read minds."

He chortles, letting his head drop. Seconds later, his gaze is back on me; stronger and more intense than before. His firm lips quiver slightly when he says, "Keeley... I'm asking you to promise to say yes, when I ask you to be my wife."

My breathing quickens as my eyes dart from the heart-shaped promise ring to Nik's smiling face. I open my mouth, relieving my chattering teeth. But before I can say anything, Nik continues.

"Don't answer yet. Let me make myself clear—I love you, Keeley. Neither of us are ready for marriage now, but I want to know that you're mine ... if that's what you want."

Aw! My heart is racing and my blood is rushing through my veins. He had me with his boyish charm alone. If it weren't freezing, I'd melt into a puddle.

Eat your hearts out, women. I'm deeply sorry for anyone who's boyfriend, fiancée, or husband doesn't treat them with the kindness, thoughtfulness, and attentiveness that Nik Valentino shows for me.

"Sparky? Will you take this promise ring as a token of my love and devotion to make you my wife one day?" The pitch of his voice increases.

Still stunned, I haven't responded.

"Please don't make me ask for a third time. You're killing me."

I grab the sides of his face and rest my forehead on his. "I'm sorry to make you wait. Nik. I love you, too." His lips curve upward slightly then gradually widen into a full, beaming expression.

Easing back so I can study him, I'm thankful the worry I heard earlier is nearly gone. "And yes, my Italian Dreamboat, I promise to accept an engagement ring when you offer one."

The feather-light kiss he gives me isn't enough. "Um. I might be missing something, but teenagers are supposed to kiss a lot. What was that?"

Boisterous laughter flies out of him. "We have an audience." He jerks his head toward the window.

"D'oh." I should have known. My hands cover my face as heat rises to my cheeks as my family rushes toward us, seemingly unaffected by the frigid weather.

"Does this mean we don't have to deal with any more grumpiness from you?" EJ jeers.

I stick my tongue out like the responsible seventeen-year-old that I am. "I make no promises."

"Good luck, Nik. She's your problem now."

I scoff. "What? It's a promise ring. You're stuck with me for a while longer."

EJ covers his mouth with the back of his hand and whisper yells, "Still your problem, bro."

I roll my eyes.

"Leave her alone. She's still recovering." Nik comes to her defense.

"Yup, that'll be her excuse for the next month." EJ winks at me.

"Love you too, bro."

My dad kneels next to me. "Are you happy?" I nod, my hair bobbing with the motion. "That's all I want and I believe Nik will take good care of you, but if he doesn't, let me know and I'll set him straight."

For the first time in her seventeen years, Keeley feels like her dad cares about her. Hopefully if she ever does need him for anything, he'll show up.

"Don't scare the boy away," Mom says, squeezing between dad and me to steal hugs—one from me and then Nik. "I have some incredibly important advice for you, something that could change your life."

"Okay," Nik's voice cracks.

"Never give my daughter a weak kiss like that again. It will ruin your marriage before you even get started."

"Mom!" Keeley shrieks.

Nik runs his hand through his hair. "But I knew you were all watching."

"That makes sense. You had performance anxiety." EJ mocks like he's a counselor or older than Nik and me.

"EJ, that's enough." Dad's stern tone makes me laugh, probably because I've never heard that tone directed toward my brother before.

"Come on, boys. Let's give them some privacy."

I feel the blush rising to my cheeks again.

"What is it with you and Keeley? We are men, not boys," EJ protests.

"You're my boys; let's move."

My dad remains still, his silence heavy against the sweet chirping birds.

"Son..." I look up; he's talking to Nik. Melt my heart. "My wife is a genius when it comes to relationships. She has put up with me all these years, so I'd listen to her. Give your girl a real kiss, but remember, if you hurt her; I'll hurt you." He smiles and turns away, trying (but failing, based on Nik's slightly open mouth and wide eyes) to ease the scariness behind his words.

"Woo hoo!" Nik hollers before his lips crash onto mine. My heart soars, a joyous symphony responding to the vibrant melody of his excitement. He is the man I envision growing old with, but for now, we have an entire journey ahead of us.

Starting with these letters.

THANK YOU FOR READING Nik and Keeley's story. Please consider sharing your thoughts on Amazon, Goodreads, and Bookbub.

Are you ready for another couple from Cumberland Christian Prep School? EJ is single as a Pringle again, but he's Mr. Personality, so I'm sure he'll have a long line of volunteers to take Liz's place. All Isabella will tell for now is that EJ and Gracie's story has a reverse Grumpy/Sunshine trope.

How About a Review?

About the Author

Karen Tucci, a public school teacher by profession, now tutors writing students online and homeschools her two children while she writes fun closed-door romance, she hopes everyone likes to read.

A native of Maine, she has trekked miles of the Pine Tree State and visited countless others. It is through her life experiences that the basis for her romance stories develop. One of her favorite things to say when out adventuring is, "...that is definitely going in my next book!"

Connect with Karen:

https://www.trueheartromance.com

Instagram

Goodreads

Bookbub

Amazon

Isabella Tucci, a homeschooled freshmen, is trying to make her mark in the world by sharing God through her kindness and compassion. When she's not reading or writing EJ's story, she spends her time writing lyrics and composing the music. Want to hear her sing cover songs? Follow her on Instagram

www.ingramcontent.com/pod-product-compliance
Lightning Source LLC
Chambersburg PA
CBHW032255310726
48973CB00008B/2416